The Short Stories of H. Rider Haggard

VOLUME I

Sir Henry Rider Haggard, KBE was born on June 22nd, 1856 at Bradenham in Norfolk, England.

After his education he was pushed towards an Army career but failed the entrance exam. Next Haggard was positioned to work for the British Foreign Office but he seems not to have sat that exam. Using family connections, he was sent to Southern Africa by his father in search of a further opportunity of a career.

Haggard spent six years there before a return to England and marriage. He had begun to write and publish some non-fiction in Africa but it was only after studying Law in the hope it might prove to be the proper career his father wanted for him that Haggard began to write fiction, using his African experiences as the basis.

His first fiction was published in 1885 and the following year King Solomon's Mines was published. It was a phenomenal success. His career was set.

Haggard wrote well and wrote often. He managed to sympathise with the local populations even though they were exploited and manipulated by Europeans intent on amassing fortunes in money, people and resources. His writing career covered the great sprint to Empire of several European powers and both reflects and criticizes these events through his well-loved characters including Allan Quatermain and Ayesha.

In his later years Haggard pursued much in the way social reform as well as standing for Parliament and writing a great many letters to The Times.

Henry Rider Haggard died on May 14th, 1925 at the age of 68. His ashes were buried at Ditchingham Church.

Index of Contents

HUNTER QUATERMAIN'S STORY

Sir Henry Curtis, as everybody acquainted with him knows, is one of the most hospitable men on earth. It was in the course of the enjoyment of his hospitality at his place in Yorkshire the other day that I heard the hunting story which I am now about to transcribe. Many of those who read it will no doubt have heard some of the strange rumours that are flying about to the effect that Sir Henry Curtis and his friend Captain Good, R.N., recently found a vast treasure of diamonds out in the heart of Africa, supposed to have been hidden by the Egyptians, or King Solomon, or some other antique people. I first saw the matter alluded to in a paragraph in one of the society papers the day before I started for Yorkshire to pay my visit to Curtis, and arrived, needless to say, burning with curiosity; for there is something very fascinating to the mind in the idea of hidden treasure. When I reached the Hall, I at once asked Curtis about it, and he did not deny the truth of the story; but on my pressing him to tell it he would not, nor would Captain Good, who was also staying in the house.

"You would not believe me if I did," Sir Henry said, with one of the hearty laughs which seem to come right out of his great lungs. "You must wait till Hunter Quatermain comes; he will arrive here from Africa to-night, and I am not going to say a word about the matter, or Good either, until he turns up. Quatermain was with us all through; he has known about the business for years and years, and if it had not been for him we should not have been here to-day. I am going to meet him presently."

I could not get a word more out of him, nor could anybody else, though we were all dying of curiosity, especially some of the ladies. I shall never forget how they looked in the drawing-room before dinner when Captain Good produced a great rough diamond, weighing fifty carats or more, and told them that he had many larger than that. If ever I saw curiosity and envy printed on fair faces, I saw them then.

It was just at this moment that the door was opened, and Mr. Allan Quatermain announced, whereupon Good put the diamond into his pocket, and sprang at a little man who limped shyly into the room, convoyed by Sir Henry Curtis himself.

"Here he is, Good, safe and sound," said Sir Henry, gleefully. "Ladies and gentlemen, let me introduce you to one of the oldest hunters and the very best shot in Africa, who has killed more elephants and lions than any other man alive."

Everybody turned and stared politely at the curious-looking little lame man, and though his size was insignificant, he was quite worth staring at. He had short grizzled hair, which stood about an inch above his head like the bristles of a brush, gentle brown eyes, that seemed to notice everything, and a withered face, tanned to the colour of mahogany from exposure to the weather. He spoke, too, when he returned Good's enthusiastic greeting, with a curious little accent, which made his speech noticeable.

It so happened that I sat next to Mr. Allan Quatermain at dinner, and, of course, did my best to draw him; but he was not to be drawn. He admitted that he had recently been a long journey into the interior of Africa with Sir Henry Curtis and Captain Good, and that they had found treasure, and then politely turned the subject and began to ask me questions about England, where he had never been before— that is, since he came to years of discretion. Of course, I did not find this very interesting, and so cast about for some means to bring the conversation round again.

Now, we were dining in an oak-panelled vestibule, and on the wall opposite to me were fixed two gigantic elephant tusks, and under them a pair of buffalo horns, very rough and knotted, showing that they came off an old bull, and having the tip of one horn split and chipped. I noticed that Hunter Quatermain's eyes kept glancing at these trophies, and took an occasion to ask him if he knew anything about them.

"I ought to," he answered, with a little laugh; "the elephant to which those tusks belonged tore one of our party right in two about eighteen months ago, and as for the buffalo horns, they were nearly my death, and were the end of a servant of mine to whom I was much attached. I gave them to Sir Henry when he left Natal some months ago;" and Mr. Quatermain sighed and turned to answer a question from the lady whom he had taken down to dinner, and who, needless to say, was also employed in trying to pump him about the diamonds.

Indeed, all round the table there was a simmer of scarcely suppressed excitement, which, when the servants had left the room, could no longer be restrained.

"Now, Mr. Quatermain," said the lady next him, "we have been kept in an agony of suspense by Sir Henry and Captain Good, who have persistently refused to tell us a word of this story about the hidden treasure till you came, and we simply can bear it no longer; so, please, begin at once."

"Yes," said everybody, "go on, please."

Hunter Quatermain glanced round the table apprehensively; he did not seem to appreciate finding himself the object of so much curiosity.

"Ladies and gentlemen," he said at last, with a shake of his grizzled head, "I am very sorry to disappoint you, but I cannot do it. It is this way. At the request of Sir Henry and Captain Good I have written down a true and plain account of King Solomon's Mines and how we found them, so you will soon be able to learn all about that wonderful adventure for yourselves; but until then I will say nothing about it, not from any wish to disappoint your curiosity, or to make myself important, but simply because the whole story partakes so much of the marvellous, that I am afraid to tell it in a piecemeal, hasty fashion, for fear I should be set down as one of those common fellows of whom there are so many in my profession, who are not ashamed to narrate things they have not seen, and even to tell wonderful stories about wild animals they have never killed. And I think that my companions in adventure, Sir Henry Curtis and Captain Good, will bear me out in what I say."

"Yes, Quatermain, I think you are quite right," said Sir Henry. "Precisely the same considerations have forced Good and myself to hold our tongues. We did not wish to be bracketed with—well, with other famous travellers."

There was a murmur of disappointment at these announcements.

"I believe you are all hoaxing us," said the young lady next Mr. Quatermain, rather sharply.

"Believe me," answered the old hunter, with a quaint courtesy and a little bow of his grizzled head; "though I have lived all my life in the wilderness, and amongst savages, I have neither the heart, nor the want of manners, to wish to deceive one so lovely."

Whereat the young lady, who was pretty, looked appeased.

"This is very dreadful," I broke in. "We ask for bread and you give us a stone, Mr. Quatermain. The least that you can do is to tell us the story of the tusks opposite and the buffalo horns underneath. We won't let you off with less."

"I am but a poor story-teller," put in the old hunter, "but if you will forgive my want of skill, I shall be happy to tell you, not the story of the tusks, for that is part of the history of our journey to King Solomon's Mines, but that of the buffalo horns beneath them, which is now ten years old."

"Bravo, Quatermain!" said Sir Henry. "We shall all be delighted. Fire away! Fill up your glass first."

The little man did as he was bid, took a sip of claret, and began:—"About ten years ago I was hunting up in the far interior of Africa, at a place called Gatgarra, not a great way from the Chobe River. I had with me four native servants, namely, a driver and voorlooper, or leader, who were natives of Matabeleland, a Hottentot named Hans, who had once been the slave of a Transvaal Boer, and a Zulu hunter, who for five years had accompanied me upon my trips, and whose name was Mashune. Now near Gatgarra I found a fine piece of healthy, park-like country, where the grass was very good, considering the time of year; and here I made a little camp or head-quarter settlement, from whence I went expeditions on all sides in search of game, especially elephant. My luck, however, was bad; I got but little ivory. I was therefore very glad when some natives brought me news that a large herd of elephants were feeding in a valley about thirty miles away. At first I thought of trekking down to the valley, waggon and all, but gave up the idea on hearing that it was infested with the deadly 'tsetse' fly, which is certain death to all animals, except men, donkeys, and wild game. So I reluctantly determined to leave the waggon in the charge of the Matabele leader and driver, and to start on a trip into the thorn country, accompanied only by the Hottentot Hans, and Mashune.

"Accordingly on the following morning we started, and on the evening of the next day reached the spot where the elephants were reported to be. But here again we were met by ill luck. That the elephants had been there was evident enough, for their spoor was plentiful, and so were other traces of their presence in the shape of mimosa trees torn out of the ground, and placed topsy-turvy on their flat crowns, in order to enable the great beasts to feed on their sweet roots; but the elephants themselves were conspicuous by their absence. They had elected to move on. This being so, there was only one thing to do, and that was to move after them, which we did, and a pretty hunt they led us. For a fortnight or more we dodged about after those elephants, coming up with them on two occasions, and a splendid herd they were—only, however, to lose them again. At length we came up with them a third time, and I managed to shoot one bull, and then they started off again, where it was useless to try and follow them. After this I gave it up in disgust, and we made the best of our way back to the camp, not in the sweetest of tempers, carrying the tusks of the elephant I had shot.

"It was on the afternoon of the fifth day of our tramp that we reached the little koppie overlooking the spot where the waggon stood, and I confess that I climbed it with a pleasurable sense of home-coming, for his waggon is the hunter's home, as much as his house is that of the civilized person. I reached the top of the koppie, and looked in the direction where the friendly white tent of the waggon should be, but there was no waggon, only a black burnt plain stretching away as far as the eye could reach. I rubbed my eyes, looked again, and made out on the spot of the camp, not my waggon, but some charred beams of wood. Half wild with grief and anxiety, followed by Hans and Mashune, I ran at full speed down the slope of the koppie, and across the space of plain below to the spring of water, where my camp had been. I was soon there, only to find that my worst suspicions were confirmed.

"The waggon and all its contents, including my spare guns and ammunition, had been destroyed by a grass fire.

"Now before I started, I had left orders with the driver to burn off the grass round the camp, in order to guard against accidents of this nature, and here was the reward of my folly: a very proper illustration of the necessity, especially where natives are concerned, of doing a thing one's self if one wants it done at all. Evidently the lazy rascals had not burnt round the waggon; most probably, indeed, they had themselves carelessly fired the tall and resinous tambouki grass near by; the wind had driven the flames on to the waggon tent, and there was quickly an end of the matter. As for the driver and leader, I know not what became of them: probably fearing my anger, they bolted, taking the oxen with them. I have never seen them from that hour to this.

"I sat down on the black veldt by the spring, and gazed at the charred axles and disselboom of my waggon, and I can assure you, ladies and gentlemen, I felt inclined to weep. As for Mashune and Hans they cursed away vigorously, one in Zulu and the other in Dutch. Ours was a pretty position. We were nearly 300 miles away from Bamangwato, the capital of Khama's country, which was the nearest spot where we could get any help, and our ammunition, spare guns, clothing, food, and everything else, were all totally destroyed. I had just what I stood in, which was a flannel shirt, a pair of 'veldt-schoons,' or shoes of raw hide, my eight-bore rifle, and a few cartridges. Hans and Mashune had also each a Martini rifle and some cartridges, not many. And it was with this equipment that we had to undertake a journey of 300 miles through a desolate and almost uninhabited region. I can assure you that I have rarely been in a worse position, and I have been in some queer ones. However, these things are the natural incidents of a hunter's life, and the only thing to do was to make the best of them.

"Accordingly, after passing a comfortless night by the remains of my waggon, we started next morning on our long journey towards civilization. Now if I were to set to work to tell you all the troubles and incidents of that dreadful journey I should keep you listening here till midnight; so I will, with your permission, pass on to the particular adventure of which the pair of buffalo horns opposite are the melancholy memento.

"We had been travelling for about a month, living and getting along as best we could, when one evening we camped some forty miles from Bamangwato. By this time we were indeed in a melancholy plight, footsore, half starved, and utterly worn out; and, in addition, I was suffering from a sharp attack of fever, which half blinded me and made me weak as a babe. Our ammunition, too, was exhausted; I had only one cartridge left for my eight-bore rifle, and Hans and Mashune, who were armed with Martini Henrys, had three between them. It was about an hour from sundown when we halted and lit a fire—for luckily we had still a few matches. It was a charming spot to camp, I remember. Just off the game track we were following was a little hollow, fringed about with flat-crowned mimosa trees, and at the bottom of the hollow, a spring of clear water welled up out of the earth, and formed a pool, round the edges of which grew an abundance of watercresses of an exactly similar kind to those which were handed round the table just now. Now we had no food of any kind left, having that morning devoured the last remains of a little oribé antelope, which I had shot two days previously. Accordingly Hans, who was a better shot than Mashune, took two of the three remaining Martini cartridges, and started out to see if he could not kill a buck for supper. I was too weak to go myself.

"Meanwhile Mashune employed himself in dragging together some dead boughs from the mimosa trees to make a sort of 'skerm,' or shelter for us to sleep in, about forty yards from the edge of the pool of water. We had been greatly troubled with lions in the course of our long tramp, and only on the previous night have very nearly been attacked by them, which made me nervous, especially in my weak state. Just as we had finished the skerm, or rather something which did duty for one, Mashune and I heard a shot apparently fired about a mile away.

"'Hark to it!' sung out Mashune in Zulu, more, I fancy, by way of keeping his spirits up than for any other reason—for he was a sort of black Mark Tapley, and very cheerful under difficulties. 'Hark to the wonderful sound with which the "Maboona" (the Boers) shook our fathers to the ground at the Battle of the Blood River. We are hungry now, my father; our stomachs are small and withered up like a dried ox's paunch, but they will soon be full of good meat. Hans is a Hottentot, and an "umfagozan," that is, a low fellow, but he shoots straight—ah! he certainly shoots straight. Be of a good heart, my father, there will soon be meat upon the fire, and we shall rise up men.'

"And so he went on talking nonsense till I told him to stop, because he made my head ache with his empty words.

"Shortly after we heard the shot the sun sank in his red splendour, and there fell upon earth and sky the great hush of the African wilderness. The lions were not up as yet, they would probably wait for the moon, and the birds and beasts were all at rest. I cannot describe the intensity of the quiet of the night: to me in my weak state, and fretting as I was over the non-return of the Hottentot Hans, it seemed almost ominous—as though Nature were brooding over some tragedy which was being enacted in her sight.

"It was quiet—quiet as death, and lonely as the grave.

"'Mashune,' I said at last, 'where is Hans? my heart is heavy for him.'

"'Nay, my father, I know not; mayhap he is weary, and sleeps, or mayhap he has lost his way.'

"'Mashune, art thou a boy to talk folly to me?' I answered. 'Tell me, in all the years thou hast hunted by my side, didst thou ever know a Hottentot to lose his path or to sleep upon the way to camp?'

"'Nay, Macumazahn' (that, ladies, is my native name, and means the man who 'gets up by night,' or who 'is always awake'), 'I know not where he is.'

"But though we talked thus, we neither of us liked to hint at what was in both our minds, namely, that misfortunate had overtaken the poor Hottentot.

"'Mashune,' I said at last, 'go down to the water and bring me of those green herbs that grow there. I am hungered, and must eat something.'

"'Nay, my father; surely the ghosts are there; they come out of the water at night, and sit upon the banks to dry themselves. An Isanusi told it me.'

Isanusi, witch-finder.

"Mashune was, I think, one of the bravest men I ever knew in the daytime, but he had a more than civilized dread of the supernatural.

"'Must I go myself, thou fool?' I said, sternly.

"'Nay, Macumazahn, if thy heart yearns for strange things like a sick woman, I go, even if the ghosts devour me.'

"And accordingly he went, and soon returned with a large bundle of watercresses, of which I ate greedily.

"'Art thou not hungry?' I asked the great Zulu presently, as he sat eyeing me eating.

"'Never was I hungrier, my father.'

"'Then eat,' and I pointed to the watercresses.

"'Nay, Macumazahn, I cannot eat those herbs.'

"'If thou dost not eat thou wilt starve: eat, Mashune.'

"He stared at the watercresses doubtfully for a while, and at last seized a handful and crammed them into his mouth, crying out as he did so, 'Oh, why was I born that I should live to feed on green weeds like an ox? Surely if my mother could have known it she would have killed me when I was born!' and so he went on lamenting between each fistful of watercresses till all were finished, when he declared that he was full indeed of stuff, but it lay very cold on his stomach, 'like snow upon a mountain.' At any other time I should have laughed, for it must be admitted he had a ludicrous way of putting things. Zulus do not like green food.

"Just after Mashune had finished his watercress, we heard the loud 'woof! woof!' of a lion, who was evidently promenading much nearer to our little skerm than was pleasant. Indeed, on looking into the darkness and listening intently, I could hear his snoring breath, and catch the light of his great yellow eyes. We shouted loudly, and Mashune threw some sticks on the fire to frighten him, which apparently had the desired effect, for we saw no more of him for a while.

"Just after we had had this fright from the lion, the moon rose in her fullest splendour, throwing a robe of silver light over all the earth. I have rarely seen a more beautiful moonrise. I remember that sitting in the skerm I could with ease read faint pencil notes in my pocket-book. As soon as the moon was up game began to trek down to the water just below us. I could, from where I sat, see all sorts of them passing along a little ridge that ran to our right, on their way to the drinking place. Indeed, one buck—a large eland—came within twenty yards of the skerm, and stood at gaze, staring at it suspiciously, his beautiful head and twisted horns standing out clearly against the sky. I had, I recollect, every mind to have a pull at him on the chance of providing ourselves with a good supply of beef; but remembering that we had but two cartridges left, and the extreme uncertainty of a shot by moonlight, I at length decided to refrain. The eland presently moved on to the water, and a minute or two afterwards there arose a great sound of splashing, followed by the quick fall of galloping hoofs.

"'What's that, Mashune?' I asked.

"'That dam lion; buck smell him,' replied the Zulu in English, of which he had a very superficial knowledge.

"Scarcely were the words out of his mouth before we heard a sort of whine over the other side of the pool, which was instantly answered by a loud coughing roar close to us.

"'By Jove!' I said, 'there are two of them. They have lost the buck; we must look out they don't catch us.' And again we made up the fire, and shouted, with the result that the lions moved off.

"'Mashune,' I said, 'do you watch till the moon gets over that tree, when it will be the middle of the night. Then wake me. Watch well, now, or the lions will be picking those worthless bones of yours before you are three hours older. I must rest a little, or I shall die.'

"'Koos!' (chief), answered the Zulu. 'Sleep, my father, sleep in peace; my eyes shall be open as the stars; and like the stars watch over you.'

"Although I was so weak, I could not at once follow his advice. To begin with, my head ached with fever, and I was torn with anxiety as to the fate of the Hottentot Hans; and, indeed, as to our own fate, left with sore feet, empty stomachs, and two cartridges, to find our way to Bamangwato, forty miles off. Then the mere sensation of knowing that there are one or more hungry lions prowling round you somewhere in the dark is disquieting, however well one may be used to it, and, by keeping the attention on the stretch, tends to prevent one from sleeping. In addition to all these troubles, too, I was, I remember, seized with a dreadful longing for a pipe of tobacco, whereas, under the circumstances, I might as well have longed for the moon.

"At last, however, I fell into an uneasy sleep as full of bad dreams as a prickly pear is of points, one of which, I recollect, was that I was setting my naked foot upon a cobra which rose upon its tail and hissed my name, 'Macumazahn,' into my ear. Indeed, the cobra hissed with such persistency that at last I roused myself.

"'Macumazahn, nanzia, nanzia!' (there, there!) whispered Mashune's voice into my drowsy ears. Raising myself, I opened my eyes, and I saw Mashune kneeling by my side and pointing towards the water. Following the line of his outstretched hand, my eyes fell upon a sight that made me jump, old hunter as I was even in those days. About twenty paces from the little skerm was a large ant-heap, and on the summit of the ant-heap, her four feet rather close together, so as to find standing space, stood the massive form of a big lioness. Her head was towards the skerm, and in the bright moonlight I saw her lower it and lick her paws.

"Mashune thrust the Martini rifle into my hands, whispering that it was loaded. I lifted it and covered the lioness, but found that even in that light I could not make out the foresight of the Martini. As it would be madness to fire without doing so, for the result would probably be that I should wound the lioness, if, indeed, I did not miss her altogether, I lowered the rifle; and, hastily tearing a fragment of paper from one of the leaves of my pocket-book, which I had been consulting just before I went to sleep, I proceeded to fix it on to the front sight. But all this took a little time, and before the paper was satisfactorily arranged, Mashune again gripped me by the arm, and pointed to a dark heap under the shade of a small mimosa tree which grew not more than ten paces from the skerm.

"'Well, what is it?' I whispered; 'I can see nothing.'

"'It is another lion,' he answered.

"'Nonsense! thy heart is dead with fear, thou seest double;' and I bent forward over the edge of the surrounding fence, and stared at the heap.

"Even as I said the words, the dark mass rose and stalked out into the moonlight. It was a magnificent, black-maned lion, one of the largest I had ever seen. When he had gone two or three steps he caught sight of me, halted, and stood there gazing straight towards us;—he was so close that I could see the firelight reflected in his wicked, greenish eyes.

"'Shoot, shoot!' said Mashune. 'The devil is coming—he is going to spring!'

"I raised the rifle, and got the bit of paper on the foresight, straight on to a little path of white hair just where the throat is set into the chest and shoulders. As I did so, the lion glanced back over his shoulder, as, according to my experience, a lion nearly always does before he springs. Then he dropped his body a little, and I saw his big paws spread out upon the ground as he put his weight on them to gather purchase. In haste I pressed the trigger of the Martini, and not a moment too soon; for, as I did so, he was in the act of springing. The report of the rifle rang out sharp and clear on the intense silence of the night, and in another second the great brute had landed on his head within four feet of us, and rolling over and over towards us, was sending the bushes which composed our little fence flying with convulsive strokes of his great paws. We sprang out of the other side of the 'skerm,' and he rolled on to it and into it and then right through the fire. Next he raised himself and sat upon his haunches like a great dog, and began to roar. Heavens! how he roared! I never heard anything like it before or since. He kept filling his lungs with air, and then emitting it in the most heart-shaking volumes of sound. Suddenly, in the middle of one of the loudest roars, he rolled over on to his side and lay still, and I knew that he was dead. A lion generally dies upon his side.

"With a sigh of relief I looked up towards his mate upon the ant-heap. She was standing there apparently petrified with astonishment, looking over her shoulder, and lashing her tail; but to our intense joy, when the dying beast ceased roaring, she turned, and, with one enormous bound, vanished into the night.

"Then we advanced cautiously towards the prostrate brute, Mashune droning an improvised Zulu song as he went, about how Macumazahn, the hunter of hunters, whose eyes are open by night as well as by day, put his hand down the lion's stomach when it came to devour him and pulled out his heart by the roots, &c., &c., by way of expressing his satisfaction, in his hyperbolical Zulu way, at the turn events had taken.

"There was no need for caution; the lion was as dead as though he had already been stuffed with straw. The Martini bullet had entered within an inch of the white spot I had aimed at, and travelled right through him, passing out at the right buttock, near the root of the tail. The Martini has wonderful driving power, though the shock it gives to the system is, comparatively speaking, slight, owing to the smallness of the hole it makes. But fortunately the lion is an easy beast to kill.

"I passed the rest of that night in a profound slumber, my head reposing upon the deceased lion's flank, a position that had, I thought, a beautiful touch of irony about it, though the smell of his singed hair was disagreeable. When I woke again the faint primrose lights of dawn were flushing in the eastern sky. For a moment I could not understand the chill sense of anxiety that lay like a lump of ice at my heart, till the feel and smell of the skin of the dead lion beneath my head recalled the circumstances in which we were placed. I rose, and eagerly looked round to see if I could discover any signs of Hans, who, if he had escaped accident, would surely return to us at dawn, but there were none. Then hope grew faint, and I felt that it was not well with the poor fellow. Setting Mashune to build up the fire I hastily removed the hide from the flank of the lion, which was indeed a splendid beast, and cutting off some lumps of flesh, we toasted and ate them greedily. Lions' flesh, strange as it may seem, is very good eating, and tastes more like veal than anything else.

"By the time we had finished our much-needed meal the sun was getting up, and after a drink of water and a wash at the pool, we started to try and find Hans, leaving the dead lion to the tender mercies of the hyænas. Both Mashune and myself were, by constant practice, pretty good hands at tracking, and we had not much difficulty in following the Hottentot's spoor, faint as it was. We had gone on in this way for half-an-hour or so, and were, perhaps, a mile or more from the site of our camping-place, when we discovered the spoor of a solitary bull buffalo mixed up with the spoor of Hans, and were able, from various indications, to make out that he had been tracking the buffalo. At length we reached a little glade in which there grew a stunted old mimosa thorn, with a peculiar and overhanging formation of root, under which a porcupine, or an ant-bear, or some such animal, had hollowed out a wide-lipped hole. About ten or fifteen paces from this thorn-tree there was a thick patch of bush.

"'See, Macumazahn! see!' said Mashune, excitedly, as we drew near the thorn; 'the buffalo has charged him. Look, here he stood to fire at him; see how firmly he planted his feet upon the earth; there is the mark of his crooked toe (Hans had one bent toe). Look! here the bull came like a boulder down the hill, his hoofs turning up the earth like a hoe. Hans had hit him: he bled as he came; there are the blood spots. It is all written down there, my father—there upon the earth.'

"'Yes,' I said; 'yes; but where is Hans?'

"Even as I said it Mashune clutched my arm, and pointed to the stunted thorn just by us. Even now, gentlemen, it makes me feel sick when I think of what I saw.

"For fixed in a stout fork of the tree some eight feet from the ground was Hans himself, or rather his dead body, evidently tossed there by the furious buffalo. One leg was twisted round the fork, probably in a dying convulsion. In the side, just beneath the ribs, was a great hole, from which the entrails protruded. But this was not all. The other leg hung down to within five feet of the ground. The skin and most of the flesh were gone from it. For a moment we stood aghast, and gazed at this horrifying sight. Then I understood what had happened. The buffalo, with that devilish cruelty which distinguishes the animal, had, after his enemy was dead, stood underneath his body, and licked the flesh off the pendant leg with his file-like tongue. I had heard of such a thing before, but had always treated the stories as hunters' yarns; but I had no doubt about it now. Poor Hans' skeleton foot and ankle were an ample proof.

"We stood aghast under the tree, and stared and stared at this awful sight, when suddenly our cogitations were interrupted in a painful manner. The thick bush about fifteen paces off burst asunder with a crashing sound, and uttering a series of ferocious pig-like grunts, the bull buffalo himself came charging out straight at us. Even as he came I saw the blood mark on his side where poor Hans' bullet had struck him, and also, as is often the case with particularly savage buffaloes, that his flanks had recently been terribly torn in an encounter with a lion.

"On he came, his head well up (a buffalo does not generally lower his head till he does so to strike); those great black horns—as I look at them before me, gentlemen, I seem to see them come charging at me as I did ten years ago, silhouetted against the green bush behind;—on, on!"

"With a shout Mashune bolted off sideways towards the bush. I had instinctively lifted my eight-bore, which I had in my hand. It would have been useless to fire at the buffalo's head, for the dense horns must have turned the bullet; but as Mashune bolted, the bull slewed a little, with the momentary idea of following him, and as this gave me a ghost of a chance, I let drive my only cartridge at his shoulder. The bullet struck the shoulder-blade and smashed it up, and then travelled on under the skin into his flank; but it did not stop him, though for a second he staggered.

"Throwing myself on to the ground with the energy of despair, I rolled under the shelter of the projecting root of the thorn, crushing myself as far into the mouth of the ant-bear hole as I could. In a single instant the buffalo was after me. Kneeling down on his uninjured knee—for one leg, that of which I had broken the shoulder, was swinging helplessly to and fro—he set to work to try and hook me out of the hole with his crooked horn. At first he struck at me furiously, and it was one of the blows against the base of the tree which splintered the tip of the horn in the way that you see. Then he grew more cunning, and pushed his head as far under the root as possible, made long semicircular sweeps at me, grunting furiously, and blowing saliva and hot steamy breath all over me. I was just out of reach of the horn, though every stroke, by widening the hole and making more room for his head, brought it closer to me, but every now and again I received heavy blows in the ribs from his muzzle. Feeling that I was being knocked silly, I made an effort and seizing his rough tongue, which was hanging from his jaws, I twisted it with all my force. The great brute bellowed with pain and fury, and jerked himself backwards so strongly, that he dragged me some inches further from the mouth of the hole, and again made a sweep at me, catching me this time round the shoulder-joint in the hook of his horn.

"I felt that it was all up now, and began to holloa.

"'He has got me!' I shouted in mortal terror. 'Gwasa, Mashune, gwasa!' ('Stab, Mashune, stab!').

"One hoist of the great head, and out of the hole I came like a periwinkle out of his shell. But even as I did so, I caught sight of Mashune's stalwart form advancing with his 'bangwan,' or broad stabbing assegai, raised above his head. In another quarter of a second I had fallen from the horn, and heard the blow of the spear, followed by the indescribable sound of steel shearing its way through flesh. I had fallen on my back, and, looking up, I saw that the gallant Mashune had driven the assegai a foot or more into the carcass of the buffalo, and was turning to fly.

"Alas! it was too late. Bellowing madly, and spouting blood from mouth and nostrils, the devilish brute was on him, and had thrown him up like a feather, and then gored him twice as he lay. I struggled up with some wild idea of affording help, but before I had gone a step the buffalo gave one long sighing bellow, and rolled over dead by the side of his victim.

"Mashune was still living, but a single glance at him told me that his hour had come. The buffalo's horn had driven a great hole in his right lung, and inflicted other injuries.

"I knelt down beside him in the uttermost distress, and took his hand.

"'Is he dead, Macumazahn?' he whispered. 'My eyes are blind; I cannot see.'

"'Yes, he is dead.'

"'Did the black devil hurt thee, Macumazahn?'

"'No, my poor fellow, I am not much hurt.'

"'Ow! I am glad.'

"Then came a long silence, broken only by the sound of the air whistling through the hole in his lung as he breathed.

"'Macumazahn, art thou there? I cannot feel thee.'

"'I am here, Mashune.'

"'I die, Macumazahn—the world flies round and round. I go—I go out into the dark! Surely, my father, at times in days to come—thou wilt think of Mashune who stood by thy side—when thou killest elephants, as we used—as we used—'

"They were his last words, his brave spirit passed with him. I dragged his body to the hole under the tree, and pushed it in, placing his broad assegai by him, according to the custom of his people, that he might not go defenceless on his long journey; and then, ladies—I am not ashamed to confess—I stood alone there before it, and wept like a woman."

LONG ODDS

The story which is narrated in the following pages came to me from the lips of my old friend Allan Quatermain, or Hunter Quatermain, as we used to call him in South Africa. He told it to me one evening when I was stopping with him at the place he bought in Yorkshire. Shortly after that, the death of his only son so unsettled him that he immediately left England, accompanied by two companions, his old fellow-voyagers, Sir Henry Curtis and Captain Good, and has now utterly vanished into the dark heart of Africa. He is persuaded that a white people, of which he has heard rumours all his life, exists somewhere on the highlands in the vast, still unexplored interior, and his great ambition is to find them before he dies. This is the wild quest upon which he and his companions have departed, and from which I shrewdly suspect they never will return. One letter only have I received from the old gentleman, dated from a mission station high up the Tana, a river on the east coast, about three hundred miles north of Zanzibar. In it he says that they have gone through many hardships and adventures, but are alive and well, and have found traces which go far towards making him hope that the results of their wild quest may be a "magnificent and unexampled discovery." I greatly fear, however, that all he has discovered is death; for this letter came a long while ago, and nobody has heard a single word of the party since. They have totally vanished.

It was on the last evening of my stay at his house that he told the ensuing story to me and Captain Good, who was dining with him. He had eaten his dinner and drunk two or three glasses of old port, just to help Good and myself to the end of the second bottle. It was an unusual thing for him to do, for he was a most abstemious man, having conceived, as he used to say, a great horror of drink from observing its effects upon the class of colonists—hunters, transport riders and others—amongst whom he had passed so many years of his life. Consequently the good wine took more effect on him than it would have done on most men, sending a little flush into his wrinkled cheeks, and making him talk more freely than usual.

Dear old man! I can see him now, as he went limping up and down the vestibule, with his grey hair sticking up in scrubbing-brush fashion, his shrivelled yellow face, and his large dark eyes, that were as keen as any hawk's, and yet soft as a buck's. The whole room was hung with trophies of his numerous hunting expeditions, and he had some story about every one of them, if only he could be got to tell it. Generally he would not, for he was not very fond of narrating his own adventures, but to-night the port wine made him more communicative.

"Ah, you brute!" he said, stopping beneath an unusually large skull of a lion, which was fixed just over the mantelpiece, beneath a long row of guns, its jaws distended to their utmost width. "Ah, you brute! you have given me a lot of trouble for the last dozen years, and will, I suppose to my dying day."

"Tell us the yarn, Quatermain," said Good. "You have often promised to tell me, and you never have."

"You had better not ask me to," he answered, "for it is a longish one."

"All right," I said, "the evening is young, and there is some more port."

Thus adjured, he filled his pipe from a jar of coarse-cut Boer tobacco that was always standing on the mantelpiece, and still walking up and down the room, began—

"It was, I think, in the March of '69 that I was up in Sikukuni's country. It was just after old Sequati's time, and Sikukuni had got into power—I forget how. Anyway, I was there. I had heard that the Bapedi people had brought down an enormous quantity of ivory from the interior, and so I started with a waggon-load of goods, and came straight away from Middelburg to try and trade some of it. It was a risky thing to go into the country so early, on account of the fever; but I knew that there were one or two others after that lot of ivory, so I determined to have a try for it, and take my chance of fever. I had become so tough from continual knocking about that I did not set it down at much.

"Well, I got on all right for a while. It is a wonderfully beautiful piece of bush veldt, with great ranges of mountains running through it, and round granite koppies starting up here and there, looking out like sentinels over the rolling waste of bush. But it is very hot—hot as a stew-pan—and when I was there that March, which, of course, is autumn in this part of Africa, the whole place reeked of fever. Every morning, as I trekked along down by the Oliphant River, I used to creep from the waggon at dawn and look out. But there was no river to be seen—only a long line of billows of what looked like the finest cotton wool tossed up lightly with a pitchfork. It was the fever mist. Out from among the scrub, too, came little spirals of vapour, as though there were hundreds of tiny fires alight in it—reek rising from thousands of tons of rotting vegetation. It was a beautiful place, but the beauty was the beauty of death; and all those lines and blots of vapour wrote one great word across the surface of the country, and that word was 'fever.'

"It was a dreadful year of illness that. I came, I remember, to one little kraal of Knobnoses, and went up to it to see if I could get some 'maas', or curdled butter-milk, and a few mealies. As I drew near I was struck with the silence of the place. No children began to chatter, and no dogs barked. Nor could I see any native sheep or cattle. The place, though it had evidently been inhabited of late, was as still as the bush round it, and some guinea-fowl got up out of the prickly pear bushes right at the kraal gate. I remember that I hesitated a little before going in, there was such an air of desolation about the spot. Nature never looks desolate when man has not yet laid his hand upon her breast; she is only lonely. But when man has been, and has passed away, then she looks desolate.

"Well, I passed into the kraal, and went up to the principal hut. In front of the hut was something with an old sheep-skin kaross thrown over it. I stooped down and drew off the rug, and then shrank back amazed, for under it was the body of a young woman recently dead. For a moment I thought of turning back, but my curiosity overcame me; so going past the dead woman, I went down on my hands and knees and crept into the hut. It was so dark that I could not see anything, though I could smell a great deal, so I lit a match. It was a 'tandstickor' match, and burnt slowly and dimly, and as the light gradually increased I made out what I took to be a family of people, men, women, and children, fast asleep. Presently it burnt up brightly, and I saw that they too, five of them altogether, were quite dead. One was a baby. I dropped the match in a hurry, and was making my way from the hut as quick as I could go, when I caught sight of two bright eyes staring out of a corner. Thinking it was a wild cat, or some such animal, I redoubled my haste, when suddenly a voice near the eyes began first to mutter, and then to send up a succession of awful yells.

"Hastily I lit another match, and perceived that the eyes belonged to an old woman, wrapped up in a greasy leather garment. Taking her by the arm, I dragged her out, for she could not, or would not, come by herself, and the stench was overpowering me. Such a sight as she was—a bag of bones, covered over with black, shrivelled parchment. The only white thing about her was her wool, and she seemed to be pretty well dead except for her eyes and her voice. She thought that I was a devil come to take her, and that is why she yelled so. Well, I got her down to the waggon, and gave her a 'tot' of Cape smoke, and then, as soon as it was ready, poured about a pint of beef-tea down her throat, made from the flesh of a blue vilderbeeste I had killed the day before, and after that she brightened up wonderfully. She could talk Zulu—indeed, it turned out that she had run away from Zululand in T'Chaka's time—and she told me that all the people whom I had seen had died of fever. When they had died the other inhabitants of the kraal had taken the cattle and gone away, leaving the poor old woman, who was helpless from age and infirmity, to perish of starvation or disease, as the case might be. She had been sitting there for three days among the bodies when I found her. I took her on to the next kraal, and gave the headman a blanket to look after her, promising him another if I found her well when I came back. I remember that he was much astonished at my parting with two blankets for the sake of such a worthless old creature. 'Why did I not leave her in the bush?' he asked. Those people carry the doctrine of the survival of the fittest to its extreme, you see.

"It was the night after I had got rid of the old woman that I made my first acquaintance with my friend yonder," and he nodded towards the skull that seemed to be grinning down at us in the shadow of the wide mantelshelf. "I had trekked from dawn till eleven o'clock—a long trek—but I wanted to get on, and had turned the oxen out to graze, sending the voorlooper to look after them, my intention being to inspan again about six o'clock, and trek with the moon till ten. Then I got into the waggon and had a good sleep till half-past two or so in the afternoon, when I rose and cooked some meat, and had my dinner, washing it down with a pannikin of black coffee—for it was difficult to get preserved milk in those days. Just as I had finished, and the driver, a man called Tom, was washing up the things, in comes the young scoundrel of a voorlooper driving one ox before him.

"'Where are the other oxen?' I asked.

"'Koos!' he said, 'Koos! the other oxen have gone away. I turned my back for a minute, and when I looked round again they were all gone except Kaptein, here, who was rubbing his back against a tree.'

"'You mean that you have been asleep, and let them stray, you villain. I will rub your back against a stick,' I answered, feeling very angry, for it was not a pleasant prospect to be stuck up in that fever trap for a week or so while we were hunting for the oxen. 'Off you go, and you too, Tom, and mind you don't come back till you have found them. They have trekked back along the Middelburg Road, and are a dozen miles off by now, I'll be bound. Now, no words; go both of you.'

"Tom, the driver, swore, and caught the lad a hearty kick, which he richly deserved, and then, having tied old Kaptein up to the disselboom with a reim, they took their assegais and sticks, and started. I would have gone too, only I knew that somebody must look after the waggon, and I did not like to leave either of the boys with it at night. I was in a very bad temper, indeed, although I was pretty well used to these sort of occurrences, and soothed myself by taking a rifle and going to kill something. For a couple of hours I poked about without seeing anything that I could get a shot at, but at last, just as I was again within seventy yards of the waggon, I put up an old Impala ram from behind a mimosa thorn. He ran straight for the waggon, and it was not till he was passing within a few feet of it that I could get a decent shot at him. Then I pulled, and caught him half-way down the spine. Over he went, dead as a door-nail, and a pretty shot it was, though I ought not to say it. This little incident put me into rather a better humour, especially as the buck had rolled right against the after-part of the waggon, so I had only to gut him, fix a reim round his legs, and haul him up. By the time I had done this the sun was down, and the full moon was up, and a beautiful moon it was. And then there came that wonderful hush which sometimes falls over the African bush in the early hours of the night. No beast was moving, and no bird called. Not a breath of air stirred the quiet trees, and the shadows did not even quiver, they only grew. It was very oppressive and very lonely, for there was not a sign of the cattle or the boys. I was quite thankful for the society of old Kaptein, who was lying down contentedly against the disselboom, chewing the cud with a good conscience.

"Presently, however, Kaptein began to get restless. First he snorted, then he got up and snorted again. I could not make it out, so like a fool I got down off the waggon-box to have a look round, thinking it might be the lost oxen coming.

"Next instant I regretted it, for all of a sudden I heard a roar and saw something yellow flash past me and light on poor Kaptein. Then came a bellow of agony from the ox, and a crunch as the lion put his teeth through the poor brute's neck, and I began to understand what had happened. My rifle was in the waggon, and my first thought being to get hold of it, I turned and made a bolt for the box. I got my foot up on the wheel and flung my body forward on to the waggon, and there I stopped as if I were frozen, and no wonder, for as I was about to spring up I heard the lion behind me, and next second I felt the brute, ay, as plainly as I can feel this table. I felt him, I say, sniffing at my left leg that was hanging down.

"My word! I did feel queer; I don't think that I ever felt so queer before. I dared not move for the life of me, and the odd thing was that I seemed to lose power over my leg, which developed an insane sort of inclination to kick out of its own mere motion—just as hysterical people want to laugh when they ought to be particularly solemn. Well, the lion sniffed and sniffed, beginning at my ankle and slowly nosing away up to my thigh. I thought that he was going to get hold then, but he did not. He only growled softly, and went back to the ox. Shifting my head a little I got a full view of him. He was about the biggest lion I ever saw, and I have seen a great many, and he had a most tremendous black mane. What his teeth were like you can see—look there, pretty big ones, ain't they? Altogether he was a magnificent animal, and as I lay sprawling on the fore-tongue of the waggon, it occurred to me that he would look uncommonly well in a cage. He stood there by the carcass of poor Kaptein, and deliberately disembowelled him as neatly as a butcher could have done. All this while I dared not move, for he kept lifting his head and keeping an eye on me as he licked his bloody chops. When he had cleaned Kaptein out he opened his mouth and roared, and I am not exaggerating when I say that the sound shook the waggon. Instantly there came back an answering roar.

"'Heavens!' I thought, 'there is his mate.'

"Hardly was the thought out of my head when I caught sight in the moonlight of the lioness bounding along through the long grass, and after her a couple of cubs about the size of mastiffs. She stopped within a few feet of my head, and stood, waved her tail, and fixed me with her glowing yellow eyes; but just as I thought that it was all over she turned and began to feed on Kaptein, and so did the cubs. There were the four of them within eight feet of me, growling and quarrelling, rending and tearing, and crunching poor Kaptein's bones; and there I lay shaking with terror, and the cold perspiration pouring out of me, feeling like another Daniel come to judgment in a new sense of the phrase. Presently the cubs had eaten their fill, and began to get restless. One went round to the back of the waggon and pulled at the Impala buck that hung there, and the other came round my way and commenced the sniffing game at my leg. Indeed, he did more than that, for, my trouser being hitched up a little, he began to lick the bare skin with his rough tongue. The more he licked the more he liked it, to judge from his increased vigour and the loud purring noise he made. Then I knew that the end had come, for in another second his file-like tongue would have rasped through the skin of my leg—which was luckily pretty tough—and have drawn the blood, and then there would be no chance for me. So I just lay there and thought of my sins, and prayed to the Almighty, and reflected that after all life was a very enjoyable thing.

"Then of a sudden I heard a crashing of bushes and the shouting and whistling of men, and there were the two boys coming back with the cattle, which they had found trekking along all together. The lions lifted their heads and listened, then bounded off without a sound—and I fainted.

"The lions came back no more that night, and by the next morning my nerves had got pretty straight again; but I was full of wrath when I thought of all that I had gone through at the hands, or rather noses, of those four brutes, and of the fate of my after-ox Kaptein. He was a splendid ox, and I was very fond of him. So wroth was I that like a fool I determined to attack the whole family of them. It was worthy of a greenhorn out on his first hunting trip; but I did it nevertheless. Accordingly after breakfast, having rubbed some oil upon my leg, which was very sore from the cub's tongue, I took the driver, Tom, who did not half like the business, and having armed myself with an ordinary double No. 12 smoothbore, the first breechloader I ever had, I started. I took the smoothbore because it shot a bullet very well; and my experience has been that a round ball from a smoothbore is quite as effective against a lion as an express bullet. The lion is soft, and not a difficult animal to finish if you hit him anywhere in the body. A buck takes far more killing.

"Well, I started, and the first thing I set to work to do was to try to discover whereabouts the brutes lay up for the day. About three hundred yards from the waggon was the crest of a rise covered with single mimosa trees, dotted about in a park-like fashion, and beyond this lay a stretch of open plain running down to a dry pan, or water-hole, which covered about an acre of ground, and was densely clothed with reeds, now in the sere and yellow leaf. From the further edge of this pan the ground sloped up again to a great cleft, or nullah, which had been cut out by the action of the water, and was pretty thickly sprinkled with bush, amongst which grew some large trees, I forget of what sort.

"It at once struck me that the dry pan would be a likely place to find my friends in, as there is nothing a lion is fonder of than lying up in reeds, through which he can see things without being seen himself. Accordingly thither I went and prospected. Before I had got half-way round the pan I found the remains of a blue vilderbeeste that had evidently been killed within the last three or four days and partially devoured by lions; and from other indications about I was soon assured that if the family were not in the pan that day they spent a good deal of their spare time there. But if there, the question was how to get them out; for it was clearly impossible to think of going in after them unless one was quite determined to commit suicide. Now there was a strong wind blowing from the direction of the waggon, across the reedy pan towards the bush-clad kloof or donga, and this first gave me the idea of firing the reeds, which, as I think I told you, were pretty dry. Accordingly Tom took some matches and began starting little fires to the left, and I did the same to the right. But the reeds were still green at the bottom, and we should never have got them well alight had it not been for the wind, which grew stronger and stronger as the sun climbed higher, and forced the fire into them. At last, after half-an-hour's trouble, the flames got a hold, and began to spread out like a fan, whereupon I went round to the further side of the pan to wait for the lions, standing well out in the open, as we stood at the copse to-day where you shot the woodcock. It was a rather risky thing to do, but I used to be so sure of my shooting in those days that I did not so much mind the risk. Scarcely had I got round when I heard the reeds parting before the onward rush of some animal. 'Now for it,' said I. On it came. I could see that it was yellow, and prepared for action, when instead of a lion out bounded a beautiful reit bok which had been lying in the shelter of the pan. It must, by the way, have been a reit bok of a peculiarly confiding nature to lay itself down with the lion, like the lamb of prophesy, but I suppose the reeds were thick, and that it kept a long way off.

"Well, I let the reit bok go, and it went like the wind, and kept my eyes fixed upon the reeds. The fire was burning like a furnace now; the flames crackling and roaring as they bit into the reeds, sending spouts of fire twenty feet and more into the air, and making the hot air dance above in a way that was perfectly dazzling. But the reeds were still half green, and created an enormous quantity of smoke, which came rolling towards me like a curtain, lying very low on account of the wind. Presently, above the crackling of the fire, I heard a startled roar, then another and another. So the lions were at home.

"I was beginning to get excited now, for, as you fellows know, there is nothing in experience to warm up your nerves like a lion at close quarters, unless it is a wounded buffalo; and I became still more so when I made out through the smoke that the lions were all moving about on the extreme edge of the reeds. Occasionally they would pop their heads out like rabbits from a burrow, and then, catching sight of me standing about fifty yards away, draw them back again. I knew that it must be getting pretty warm behind them, and that they could not keep the game up for long; and I was not mistaken, for suddenly all four of them broke cover together, the old black-maned lion leading by a few yards. I never saw a more splendid sight in all my hunting experience than those four lions bounding across the veldt, overshadowed by the dense pall of smoke and backed by the fiery furnace of the burning reeds.

"I reckoned that they would pass, on their way to the bushy kloof, within about five and twenty yards of me, so, taking a long breath, I got my gun well on to the lion's shoulder—the black-maned one—so as to allow for an inch or two of motion, and catch him through the heart. I was on, dead on, and my finger was just beginning to tighten on the trigger, when suddenly I went blind—a bit of reed-ash had drifted into my right eye. I danced and rubbed, and succeeded in clearing it more or less just in time to see the tail of the last lion vanishing round the bushes up the kloof.

"If ever a man was mad I was that man. It was too bad; and such a shot in the open! However, I was not going to be beaten, so I just turned and marched for the kloof. Tom, the driver, begged and implored me not to go, but though as a general rule I never pretend to be very brave (which I am not), I was determined that I would either kill those lions or they should kill me. So I told Tom that he need not come unless he liked, but I was going; and being a plucky fellow, a Swazi by birth, he shrugged his shoulders, muttered that I was mad or bewitched, and followed doggedly in my tracks.

"We soon reached the kloof, which was about three hundred yards in length and but sparsely wooded, and then the real fun began. There might be a lion behind every bush—there certainly were four lions somewhere; the delicate question was, where. I peeped and poked and looked in every possible direction, with my heart in my mouth, and was at last rewarded by catching a glimpse of something yellow moving behind a bush. At the same moment, from another bush opposite me out burst one of the cubs and galloped back towards the burnt pan. I whipped round and let drive a snap shot that tipped him head over heels, breaking his back within two inches of the root of the tail, and there he lay helpless but glaring. Tom afterwards killed him with his assegai. I opened the breech of the gun and hurriedly pulled out the old case, which, to judge from what ensued, must, I suppose, have burst and left a portion of its fabric sticking to the barrel. At any rate, when I tried to, get in the new cartridge it would only enter half-way; and—would you believe it?—this was the moment that the lioness, attracted no doubt by the outcry of her cub, chose to put in an appearance. There she stood, twenty paces or so from me, lashing her tail and looking just as wicked as it is possible to conceive. Slowly I stepped backwards, trying to push in the new case, and as I did so she moved on in little runs, dropping down after each run. The danger was imminent, and the case would not go in. At the moment I oddly enough thought of the cartridge maker, whose name I will not mention, and earnestly hoped that if the lion got me some condign punishment would overtake him. It would not go in, so I tried to pull it out. It would not come out either, and my gun was useless if I could not shut it to use the other barrel. I might as well have had no gun.

"Meanwhile I was walking backward, keeping my eye on the lioness, who was creeping forward on her belly without a sound, but lashing her tail and keeping her eye on me; and in it I saw that she was coming in a few seconds more. I dashed my wrist and the palm of my hand against the brass rim of the cartridge till the blood poured from them—look, there are the scars of it to this day!"

Here Quatermain held up his right hand to the light and showed us four or five white cicatrices just where the wrist is set into the hand.

"But it was not of the slightest use," he went on, "the cartridge would not move. I only hope that no other man will ever be put in such an awful position. The lioness gathered herself together, and I gave myself up for lost, when suddenly Tom shouted out from somewhere in my rear—

"'You are walking on to the wounded cub; turn to the right.'

"I had the sense, dazed as I was, to take the hint, and slewing round at right-angles, but still keeping my eyes on the lioness, I continued my backward walk.

"To my intense relief, with a low growl she straightened herself, turned, and bounded further up the kloof.

"'Come on, Macumazahn,' said Tom, 'let's get back to the waggon.'

"'All right, Tom,' I answered. 'I will when I have killed those three other lions,' for by this time I was bent on shooting them as I never remember being bent on anything before or since. 'You can go if you like, or you can get up a tree.'

"He considered the position a little, and then he very wisely got up a tree. I wish that I had done the same.

"Meanwhile I had found my knife, which had an extractor in it, and succeeded after some difficulty in pulling out the cartridge which had so nearly been the cause of my death, and removing the obstruction in the barrel. It was very little thicker than a postage-stamp; certainly not thicker than a piece of writing-paper. This done, I loaded the gun, bound a handkerchief round my wrist and hand to staunch the flowing of the blood, and started on again.

"I had noticed that the lioness went into a thick green bush, or rather cluster of bushes, growing near the water, about fifty yards higher up, for there was a little stream running down the kloof, and I walked towards this bush. When I got there, however, I could see nothing, so I took up a big stone and threw it into the bushes. I believe that it hit the other cub, for out it came with a rush, giving me a broadside shot, of which I promptly availed myself, knocking it over dead. Out, too, came the lioness like a flash of light, but quick as she went I managed to put the other bullet into her ribs, so that she rolled right over three times like a shot rabbit. I instantly got two more cartridges into the gun, and as I did so the lioness rose again and came crawling towards me on her fore-paws, roaring and groaning, and with such an expression of diabolical fury on her countenance as I have not often seen. I shot her again through the chest, and she fell over on to her side quite dead.

"That was the first and last time that I ever killed a brace of lions right and left, and, what is more, I never heard of anybody else doing it. Naturally I was considerably pleased with myself, and having again loaded up, I went on to look for the black-maned beauty who had killed Kaptein. Slowly, and with the greatest care, I proceeded up the kloof, searching every bush and tuft of grass as I went. It was wonderfully exciting, work, for I never was sure from one moment to another but that he would be on me. I took comfort, however, from the reflection that a lion rarely attacks a man—rarely, I say; sometimes he does, as you will see—unless he is cornered or wounded. I must have been nearly an hour hunting after that lion. Once I thought I saw something move in a clump of tambouki grass, but I could not be sure, and when I trod out the grass I could not find him.

"At last I worked up to the head of the kloof, which made a cul-de-sac. It was formed of a wall of rock about fifty feet high. Down this rock trickled a little waterfall, and in front of it, some seventy feet from its face, rose a great piled-up mass of boulders, in the crevices and on the top of which grew ferns, grasses, and stunted bushes. This mass was about twenty-five feet high. The sides of the kloof here were also very steep. Well, I came to the top of the nullah and looked all round. No signs of the lion. Evidently I had either overlooked him further down or he had escaped right away. It was very vexatious; but still three lions were not a bad bag for one gun before dinner, and I was fain to be content. Accordingly I departed back again, making my way round the isolated pillar of boulders, beginning to feel, as I did so, that I was pretty well done up with excitement and fatigue, and should be more so before I had skinned those three lions. When I had got, as nearly as I could judge, about eighteen yards past the pillar or mass of boulders, I turned to have another look round. I have a pretty sharp eye, but I could see nothing at all.

"Then, on a sudden, I saw something sufficiently alarming. On the top of the mass of boulders, opposite to me, standing out clear against the rock beyond, was the huge black-maned lion. He had been crouching there, and now arose as though by magic. There he stood lashing his tail, just like a living reproduction of the animal on the gateway of Northumberland House that I have seen in a picture. But he did not stand long. Before I could fire—before I could do more than get the gun to my shoulder—he sprang straight up and out from the rock, and driven by the impetus of that one mighty bound came hurtling through the air towards me.

"Heavens! how grand he looked, and how awful! High into the air he flew, describing a great arch. Just as he touched the highest point of his spring I fired. I did not dare to wait, for I saw that he would clear the whole space and land right upon me. Without a sight, almost without aim, I fired, as one would fire a snap shot at a snipe. The bullet told, for I distinctly heard its thud above the rushing sound caused by the passage of the lion through the air. Next second I was swept to the ground (luckily I fell into a low, creeper-clad bush, which broke the shock), and the lion was on the top of me, and the next those great white teeth of his had met in my thigh—I heard them grate against the bone. I yelled out in agony, for I did not feel in the least benumbed and happy, like Dr. Livingstone—whom, by the way, I knew very well—and gave myself up for dead. But suddenly, at that moment, the lion's grip on my thigh loosened, and he stood over me, swaying to and fro, his huge mouth, from which the blood was gushing, wide opened. Then he roared, and the sound shook the rocks.

"To and fro he swung, and then the great head dropped on me, knocking all the breath from my body, and he was dead. My bullet had entered in the centre of his chest and passed out on the right side of the spine about half way down the back.

"The pain of my wound kept me from fainting, and as soon as I got my breath I managed to drag myself from under him. Thank heavens, his great teeth had not crushed my thigh-bone; but I was losing a great deal of blood, and had it not been for the timely arrival of Tom, with whose aid I loosed the handkerchief from my wrist and tied it round my leg, twisting it tight with a stick, I think that I should have bled to death.

"Well, it was a just reward for my folly in trying to tackle a family of lions single-handed. The odds were too long. I have been lame ever since, and shall be to my dying day; in the month of March the wound always troubles me a great deal, and every three years it breaks out raw.

"I need scarcely add that I never traded the lot of ivory at Sikukuni's. Another man got it—a German— and made five hundred pounds out of it after paying expenses. I spent the next month on the broad of my back, and was a cripple for six months after that. And now I've told you the yarn, so I will have a drop of Hollands and go to bed. Good-night to you all, good-night!"

THE MAHATMA AND THE HARE

A DREAM STORY

"Ultimately a good hare was found which took the field at . . . There the hounds pressed her, and on the hunt arriving at the edge of the cliff the hare could be seen crossing the beach and going right out to sea. A boat was procured, and the master and some others rowed out to her just as she drowned, and, bringing the body in, gave it to the hounds. A hare swimming out to sea is a sight not often witnessed."—Local paper, January 1911.

". . . A long check occurred in the latter part of this hunt, the hare having laid up in a hedgerow, from which she was at last evicted by a crack of the whip. Her next place of refuge was a horse-pond, which she tried to swim, but got stuck in the ice midway, and was sinking, when the huntsman went in after her. It was a novel sight to see huntsman and hare being lifted over a wall out of the pond, the eager pack waiting for their prey behind the wall."—Local paper, February 1911.

The author supposes that the first of the above extracts must have impressed him. At any rate, on the night after the reading of it, just as he went to sleep, or on the following morning just as he awoke, he cannot tell which, there came to him the title and the outlines of this fantasy, including the command with which it ends. With a particular clearness did he seem to see the picture of the Great White Road, "straight as the way of the Spirit, and broad as the breast of Death," and of the little Hare travelling towards the awful Gates.

Like the Mahatma of this fable, he expresses no opinion as to the merits of the controversy between the Red-faced Man and the Hare that, without search on his own part, presented itself to his mind in so odd a fashion. It is one on which anybody interested in such matters can form an individual judgment.

THE MAHATMA[*]

[*] Mahatma, "great-souled." "One of a class of persons with preter-natural powers, imagined to exist in India and Thibet."—New English Dictionary.

Everyone has seen a hare, either crouched or running in the fields, or hanging dead in a poulterer's shop, or lastly pathetic, even dreadful-looking and in this form almost indistinguishable from a skinned cat, on the domestic table. But not many people have met a Mahatma, at least to their knowledge. Not many people know even who or what a Mahatma is. The majority of those who chance to have heard the title are apt to confuse it with another, that of Mad Hatter.

This is even done of malice prepense (especially, for obvious reasons, if a hare is in any way concerned) in scorn, not in ignorance, by persons who are well acquainted with the real meaning of the word and even with its Sanscrit origin. The truth is that an incredulous Western world puts no faith in Mahatmas. To it a Mahatma is a kind of spiritual Mrs. Harris, giving an address in Thibet at which no letters are delivered. Either, it says, there is no such person, or he is a fraudulent scamp with no greater occult powers—well, than a hare.

I confess that this view of Mahatmas is one that does not surprise me in the least. I never met, and I scarcely expect to meet, an individual entitled to set "Mahatma" after his name. Certainly I have no right to do so, who only took that title on the spur of the moment when the Hare asked me how I was called, and now make use of it as a nom-de-plume. It is true there is Jorsen, by whose order, for it amounts to that, I publish this history. For aught I know Jorsen may be a Mahatma, but he does not in the least look the part.

Imagine a bluff person with a strong, hard face, piercing grey eyes, and very prominent, bushy eyebrows, of about fifty or sixty years of age. Add a Scotch accent and a meerschaum pipe, which he smokes even when he is wearing a frock coat and a tall hat, and you have Jorsen. I believe that he lives somewhere in the country, is well off, and practises gardening. If so he has never asked me to his place, and I only meet him when he comes to Town, as I understand, to visit flower-shows.

Then I always meet him because he orders me to do so, not by letter or by word of mouth but in quite a different way. Suddenly I receive an impression in my mind that I am to go to a certain place at a certain hour, and that there I shall find Jorsen. I do go, sometimes to an hotel, sometimes to a lodging, sometimes to a railway station or to the corner of a particular street and there I do find Jorsen smoking his big meerschaum pipe. We shake hands and he explains why he has sent for me, after which we talk of various things. Never mind what they are, for that would be telling Jorsen's secrets as well as my own, which I must not do.

It may be asked how I came to know Jorsen. Well, in a strange way. Nearly thirty years ago a dreadful thing happened to me. I was married and, although still young, a person of some mark in literature. Indeed even now one or two of the books which I wrote are read and remembered, although it is supposed that their author has long left the world.

The thing which happened was that my wife and our daughter were coming over from the Channel Islands, where they had been on a visit (she was a Jersey woman), and, and—well, the ship was lost, that's all. The shock broke my heart, in such a way that it has never been mended again, but unfortunately did not kill me.

Afterwards I took to drink and sank, as drunkards do. Then the river began to draw me. I had a lodging in a poor street at Chelsea, and I could hear the river calling me at night, and—I wished to die as the others had died. At last I yielded, for the drink had rotted out all my moral sense. About one o'clock of a wild, winter morning I went to a bridge I knew where in those days policemen rarely came, and listened to that call of the water.

"Come!" it seemed to say. "This world is the real hell, ending in the eternal naught. The dreams of a life beyond and of re-union there are but a demon's mocking breathed into the mortal heart, lest by its universal suicide mankind should rob him of his torture-pit. There is no truth in all your father taught you" (he was a clergyman and rather eminent in his profession), "there is no hope for man, there is nothing he can win except the deep happiness of sleep. Come and sleep."

Such were the arguments of that Voice of the river, the old, familiar arguments of desolation and despair. I leant over the parapet; in another moment I should have been gone, when I became aware that some one was standing near to me. I did not see the person because it was too dark. I did not hear him because of the raving of the wind. But I knew that he was there. So I waited until the moon shone out for a while between the edges of two ragged clouds, the shapes of which I can see to this hour. It showed me Jorsen, looking just as he does to-day, for he never seems to change—Jorsen, on whom, to my knowledge, I had not set eyes before.

"Even a year ago," he said, in his strong, rough voice, "you would not have allowed your mind to be convinced by such arguments as those which you have just heard in the Voice of the river. That is one of the worst sides of drink; it decays the reason as it does the body. You must have noticed it yourself."

I replied that I had, for I was surprised into acquiescence. Then I grew defiant and asked him what he knew of the arguments which were or were not influencing me. To my surprise—no, that is not the word—to my bewilderment, he repeated them to me one by one just as they had arisen a few minutes before in my heart. Moreover, he told me what I had been about to do, and why I was about to do it.

"You know me and my story," I muttered at last.

"No," he answered, "at least not more than I know that of many men with whom I chance to be in touch. That is, I have not met you for nearly eleven hundred years. A thousand and eighty-six, to be correct. I was a blind priest then and you were the captain of Irene's guard."

At this news I burst out laughing and the laugh did me good.

"I did not know I was so old," I said.

"Do you call that old?" answered Jorsen. "Why, the first time that we had anything to do with each other, so far as I can learn, that is, was over eight thousand years ago, in Egypt before the beginning of recorded history."

"I thought that I was mad, but you are madder," I said.

"Doubtless. Well, I am so mad that I managed to be here in time to save you from suicide, as once in the past you saved me, for thus things come round. But your rooms are near, are they not? Let us go there and talk. This place is cold and the river is always calling."

That was how I came to know Jorsen, whom I believe to be one of the greatest men alive. On this particular night that I have described he told me many things, and since then he has taught me much, me and a few others. But whether he is what is called a Mahatma I am sure I do not know. He has never claimed such a rank in my hearing, or indeed to be anything more than a man who has succeeded in winning a knowledge of his own powers out of the depths of the dark that lies behind us. Of course I mean out of his past in other incarnations long before he was Jorsen. Moreover, by degrees, as I grew fit to bear the light, he showed me something of my own, and of how the two were intertwined.

But all these things are secrets of which I have perhaps no right to speak at present. It is enough to say that Jorsen changed the current of my life on that night when he saved me from death.

For instance, from that day onwards to the present time I have never touched the drink which so nearly ruined me. Also the darkness has rolled away, and with it every doubt and fear; I know the truth, and for that truth I live. Considered from certain aspects such knowledge, I admit, is not altogether desirable. Thus it has deprived me of my interest in earthly things. Ambition has left me altogether; for years I have had no wish to succeed in the profession which I adopted in my youth, or in any other. Indeed I doubt whether the elements of worldly success still remain in me; whether they are not entirely burnt away by that fire of wisdom in which I have bathed. How can we strive to win a crown we have no longer any desire to wear? Now I desire other crowns and at times I wear them, if only for a little while. My spirit grows and grows. It is dragging at its strings.

What am I to look at? A small, white-haired man with a thin and rather plaintive face in which are set two large, dark eyes that continually seem to soften and develop. That is my picture. And what am I in the world? I will tell you. On certain days of the week I employ myself in editing a trade journal that has to do with haberdashery. On another day I act as auctioneer to a firm which imports and sells cheap Italian statuary; modern, very modern copies of the antique, florid marble vases, and so forth. Some of you who read may have passed such marts in different parts of the city, or even have dropped in and purchased a bust or a tazza for a surprisingly small sum. Perhaps I knocked it down to you, only too pleased to find a bonâ fide bidder amongst my company.

As for the rest of my time—well, I employ it in doing what good I can among the poor and those who need comfort or who are bereaved, especially among those who are bereaved, for to such I am sometimes able to bring the breath of hope that blows from another shore.

Occasionally also I amuse myself in my own fashion. Thus sure knowledge has come to me about certain epochs in the past in which I lived in other shapes, and I study those epochs, hoping that one day I may find time to write of them and of the parts I played in them. Some of these parts are extremely interesting, especially as I am of course able to contrast them with our modern modes of thought and action.

They do not all come back to me with equal clearness, the earlier lives being, as one might expect, the more difficult to recover and the comparatively recent ones the easiest. Also they seem to range over a vast stretch of time, back indeed to the days of primeval, prehistoric man. In short, I think the subconscious in some ways resembles the conscious and natural memory; that which is very far off to it grows dim and blurred, that which is comparatively close remains clear and sharp, although of course this rule is not invariable. Moreover there is foresight as well as memory. At least from time to time I seem to come in touch with future events and states of society in which I shall have my share.

I believe some thinkers hold a theory that such conditions as those of past, present, and future do not in fact exist; that everything already is, standing like a completed column between earth and heaven; that the sum is added up, the equation worked out. At times I am tempted to believe in the truth of this proposition. But if it be true, of course it remains difficult to obtain a clear view of other parts of the column than that in which we happen to find ourselves objectively conscious at any given period, and needless to say impossible to see it from base to capital.

However this may be, no individual entity pervades all the column. There are great sections of it with which that entity has nothing to do, although it always seems to appear again above. I suppose that those sections which are empty of an individual and his atmosphere represent the intervals between his lives which he spends in sleep, or in states of existence with which this world is not concerned, but of such gulfs of oblivion and states of being I know nothing.

To take a single instance of what I do know: once this spirit of mine, that now by the workings of destiny for a little while occupies the body of a fourth-rate auctioneer, and of the editor of a trade journal, dwelt in that of a Pharaoh of Egypt—never mind which Pharoah. Yes, although you may laugh and think me mad to say it, for me the legions fought and thundered; to me the peoples bowed and the secret sanctuaries were opened that I and I alone might commune with the gods; I who in the flesh and after it myself was worshipped as a god.

Well, of this forgotten Royalty of whom little is known save what a few inscriptions have to tell, there remains a portrait statue in the British Museum. Sometimes I go to look at that statue and try to recall exactly under what circumstances I caused it to be shaped, puzzling out the story bit by bit.

Not long ago I stood thus absorbed and did not notice that the hour of the closing of the great gallery had come. Still I stood and gazed and dreamt till the policeman on duty, seeing and suspecting me, came up and roughly ordered me to begone.

The man's tone angered me. I laid my hand on the foot of the statue, for it had just come back to me that it was a "Ka" image, a sacred thing, any Egyptologist will know what I mean, which for ages had sat in a chamber of my tomb. Then the Ka that clings to it eternally awoke at my touch and knew me, or so I suppose. At least I felt myself change. A new strength came into me; my shape, battered in this world's storms, put on something of its ancient dignity; my eyes grew royal. I looked at that man as Pharaoh may have looked at one who had done him insult. He saw the change and trembled—yes, trembled. I believe he thought I was some imperial ghost that the shadows of evening had caused him to mistake for man; at any rate he gasped out—

"I beg your pardon, I was obeying orders. I hope your Majesty won't hurt me. Now I think of it I have been told that things come out of these old statues in the night."

Then turning he ran, literally ran, where to I am sure I do not know, probably to seek the fellowship of some other policeman. In due course I followed, and, lifting the bar at the end of the hall, departed without further question asked. Afterwards I was very glad to think that I had done the man no injury. At the moment I knew that I could hurt him if I would, and what is more I had the desire to do so. It came to me, I suppose, with that breath of the past when I was so great and absolute. Perhaps I, or that part of me then incarnate, was a tyrant in those days, and this is why now I must be so humble. Fate is turning my pride to its hammer and beating it out of me.

For thus in the long history of the soul it serves all our vices.

THE GREAT WHITE ROAD

Now, as I have hinted, under the teaching of Jorsen, who saved me from degradation and self-murder, yes, and helped me with money until once again I could earn a livelihood, I have acquired certain knowledge and wisdom of a sort that are not common. That is, Jorsen taught me the elements of these things; he set my feet upon the path which thenceforward, having the sight, I have been able to follow for myself. How I followed it does not matter, nor could I teach others if I would.

I am no member of any mystic brotherhood, and, as I have explained, no Mahatma, although I have called myself thus for present purposes because the name is a convenient cloak. I repeat that I am ignorant if there are such people as Mahatmas, though if so I think Jorsen must be one of them. Still he never told me this. What he has told is that every individual spirit must work out its own destiny quite independently of others. Indeed, being rather fond of fine phrases, he has sometimes spoken to me of, or rather, insisted upon what he called "the lonesome splendour of the human soul," which it is our business to perfect through various lives till I can scarcely appreciate and am certainly unable to describe.

To tell the truth, the thought of this "lonesome splendour" to which it seems some of us may attain, alarms me. I have had enough of being lonesome, and I do not ask for any particular splendour. My only ambitions are to find those whom I have lost, and in whatever life I live to be of use to others. However, as I gather that the exalted condition to which Jorsen alludes is thousands of ages off for any of us, and may after all mean something quite different to what it seems to mean, the thought of it does not trouble me over much. Meanwhile what I seek is the vision of those I love.

Now I have this power. Occasionally when I am in deep sleep some part of me seems to leave my body and to be transported quite outside the world. It travels, as though I were already dead, to the Gates that all who live must pass, and there takes its stand, on the Great White Road, watching those who have been called speed by continually. Those upon the earth know nothing of that Road. Blinded by their pomps and vanities, they cannot see, they will not see it always growing towards the feet of every one of them. But I see and know. Of course you who read will say that this is but a dream of mine, and it may be. Still, if so, it is a very wonderful dream, and except for the change of the passing people, or rather of those who have been people, always very much the same.

There, straight as the way of the Spirit and broad as the breast of Death, is the Great White Road running I know not whence, up to those Gates that gleam like moonlight and are higher than the Alps. There beyond the Gates the radiant Presences move mysteriously. Thence at the appointed time the Voice cries and they are opened with a sound like to that of deepest thunder, or sometimes are burned away, while from the Glory that lies beyond flow the sweet-faced welcomers to greet those for whom they wait, bearing the cups from which they give to drink. I do not know what is in the cups, whether it be a draught of Lethe or some baptismal water of new birth, or both; but always the thirsting, world-worn soul appears to change, and then as it were to be lost in the Presence that gave the cup. At least they are lost to my sight. I see them no more.

Why do I watch those Gates, in truth or in dream, before my time? Oh! You can guess. That perchance I may behold those for whom my heart burns with a quenchless, eating fire. And once I beheld—not the mother but the child, my child, changed indeed, mysterious, wonderful, gleaming like a star, with eyes so deep that in their depths my humanity seemed to swoon.

She came forward; she knew me; she smiled and laid her finger on her lips. She shook her hair about her and in it vanished as in a cloud. Yet as she vanished a voice spoke in my heart, her voice, and the words it said were—

"Wait, our Beloved! Wait!"

Mark well. "Our Beloved," not "My Beloved." So there are others by whom I am beloved, or at least one other, and I know well who that one must be.

After this dream, perhaps I had better call it a dream, I was ill for a long while, for the joy and the glory of it overpowered me and brought me near to the death I had always sought. But I recovered, for my hour is not yet. Moreover, for a long while as we reckon time, some years indeed, I obeyed the injunction and sought the Great White Road no more. At length the longing grew too strong for me and I returned thither, but never again did the vision come. Its word was spoken, its mission was fulfilled. Yet from time to time I, a mortal, seem to stand upon the borders of that immortal Road and watch the newly dead who travel it towards the glorious Gates.

Once or twice there have been among them people whom I have known. As these pass me I appear to have the power of looking into their hearts, and there I read strange things. Sometimes they are beautiful things and sometimes ugly things. Thus I have learned that those I thought bad were really good in the main, for who can claim to be quite good? And on the other hand that those I believed to be as honest as the day—well, had their faults.

To take an example which I quote because it is so absurd. The rooms I live in were owned by a prim old woman who for more than twenty years was my landlady. She and I were great friends, indeed she tended me like a mother, and when I was so ill nursed me as perhaps few mothers would have done. Yet while I was watching on the Road suddenly she came by, and with horror I saw that during all those years she had been robbing me, taking, I am sorry to say, many things, in money, trinkets, and food. Often I had discussed with her where these articles could possibly have gone, till finally suspicion settled upon the man who cleaned the windows. Yes, and worst of all, he was prosecuted, and I gave evidence against him, or rather strengthened her evidence, on faith of which the magistrate sent him to prison for a month.

"Oh! Mrs Smithers," I said to her, "how could you do it, Mrs. Smithers?"

She stopped and looked about her terrified, so that my heart smote me and I added in haste, "Don't be frightened, Mrs. Smithers; I forgive you."

"I can't see you, sir," she exclaimed, or so I dreamed, "but there! I always knew you would."

"Yes, Mrs. Smithers," I replied; "but how about the window-cleaner who went to jail and lost his situation?"

Then she passed on or was drawn away without making any answer.

Now comes the odd part of the story. When I woke up on the following morning in my rooms, it was to be informed by the frightened maid-of-all-work that Mrs. Smithers had been found dead in her bed. Moreover, a few days later I learned from a lawyer that she had made a will leaving me everything she possessed, including the lease of her house and nearly £1000, for she had been a saving old person during all her long life.

Well, I sought out that window-cleaner and compensated him handsomely, saying that I had found I was mistaken in the evidence I gave against him. The rest of the property I kept, and I hope that it was not wrong of me to do so. It will be remembered that some of it was already my own, temporarily diverted into another channel, and for the rest I have so many to help. To be frank I do not spend much upon myself.

THE HARE

Now I have done with myself, or rather with my own insignificant present history, and come to that of the Hare. It impressed me a good deal at the time, which is not long ago, so much indeed that I communicated the facts to Jorsen. He ordered me to publish them, and what Jorsen orders must be done. I don't know why this should be, but it is so. He has authority of a sort that I am unable to define.

One night after the usual aspirations and concentration of mind, which by the way are not always successful, I passed into what occultists call spirit, and others a state of dream. At any rate I found myself upon the borders of the Great White Road, as near to the mighty Gates as I am ever allowed to come. How far that may be away I cannot tell. Perhaps it is but a few yards and perhaps it is the width of this great world, for in that place which my spirit visits time and distance do not exist. There all things are new and strange, not to be reckoned by our measures. There the sight is not our sight nor the hearing our hearing. I repeat that all things are different, but that difference I cannot describe, and if I could it would prove past comprehension.

There I sat by the borders of the Great White Road, my eyes fixed upon the Gates above which the towers mount for miles on miles, outlined against an encircling gloom with the radiance of the world beyond the worlds. Four-square they stand, those towers, and fourfold the gates that open to the denizens of other earths. But of these I have no knowledge beyond the fact that it is so in my visions.

I sat upon the borders of the Road, my eyes fixed in hope upon the Gates, though well I knew that the hope would never be fulfilled, and watched the dead go by.

They were many that night. Some plague was working in the East and unchaining thousands. The folk that it loosed were strange to me who in this particular life have seldom left England, and I studied them with curiosity; high-featured, dark-hued people with a patient air. The knowledge which I have told me that one and all they were very ancient souls who often and often had walked this Road before, and therefore, although as yet they did not know it, were well accustomed to the journey. No, I am wrong, for here and there an individual did know. Indeed one deep-eyed, wistful little woman, who carried a baby in her arms, stopped for a moment and spoke to me.

"The others cannot see you as I do," she said. "Priest of the Queen of queens, I know you well; hand in hand we climbed by the seven stairways to the altars of the moon."

"Who is the Queen of queens?" I asked.

"Have you forgotten her of the hundred names whose veils we lifted one by one; her whose breast was beauty and whose eyes were truth? In a day to come you will remember. Farewell till we walk this Road no more."

"Stay—when did we meet?"

"When our souls were young," she answered, and faded from my ken like a shadow from the sea.

After the Easterns came many others from all parts of the earth. Then suddenly appeared a company of about six hundred folk of every age and English in their looks. They were not so calm as are the majority of those who make this journey. When I read the papers a few days later I understood why. A great passenger ship had sunk suddenly in mid ocean and they were all cut off unprepared.

When, followed by a few stragglers, these had passed and gathered themselves in the red shadow beneath the gateway towers waiting for the summons, an unusual thing occurred. For a few moments the Road was left quite empty. After that last great stroke Death seemed to be resting on his laurels. When thus unpeopled it looked a very vast place like to a huge arched causeway, bordered on either side by blackness, but itself gleaming with a curious phosphorescence such as once or twice I have seen in the waters of a summer sea at night.

Presently in the very centre of this illuminated desolation, whilst it was as yet far away, something caught my eye, something so strange to the place, so utterly unfamiliar that I watched it earnestly, wondering what it might be. Nearer and nearer it came, with curious, uncertain hops; yes, a little brown object that hopped.

"Well," I said to myself, "if I were not where I am I should say that yonder thing was a hare. Only what would a hare be doing on the Great White Road? How could a hare tread the pathway of eternal souls? I must be mistaken."

So I reflected whilst still the thing hopped on, until I became certain that either I suffered from delusions, or that it was a hare; indeed a particularly fine hare, much such a one as a friend of my old landlady, Mrs. Smithers, had once sent her as a Christmas present from Norfolk, which hare I ate.

A few more hops brought it opposite to my post of observation. Here it halted as though it seemed to see me. At any rate it sat up in the alert fashion that hares have, its forepaws hanging absurdly in front of it, with one ear, on which there was a grey blotch, cocked and one dragging, and sniffed with its funny little nostrils. Then it began to talk to me. I do not mean that it really talked, but the thoughts which were in its mind were flashed on to my mind so that I understood perfectly, yes, and could answer them in the same fashion. It said, or thought, thus:—

"You are real. You are a man who yet lives beneath the sun, though how you came here I do not know. I hate men, all hares do, for men are cruel to them. Still it is a comfort in this strange place to see something one has seen before and to be able to talk even to a man, which I could never do until the change came, the dreadful change—I mean because of the way of it," and it seemed to shiver. "May I ask you some questions?"

"Certainly," I said or rather thought back.

"You are sure that they won't make you angry so that you hurt me?"

"I can't hurt you, even if I wished to do so. You are not a hare any longer, if you ever were one, but only the shadow of a hare."

"Ah! I thought as much, and that's a good thing anyhow. Tell me, Man, have you ever been torn to pieces by dogs?"

"Good gracious! no."

"Or coursed, or hunted, or caught in a trap, or shot all over your back, or twisted up in nets and choked in snares? Or have you swum out to sea to die more easily, or seen your mate and mother and father killed?"

"No, no. Please stop, Hare; your questions are very unpleasant."

"Not half so unpleasant as the things are themselves, I can assure you, Man. I will tell you my story if you like; then you can judge for yourself. But first, if you will, do you tell me why I am here. Have you seen more hares about this place?"

"Never, nor any other animals. No, I am wrong, once I saw a dog."

The Hare looked about it anxiously.

"A dog. How horrible! What was it doing? Hunting? If there are no hares here what could it be hunting? A rabbit, or a pheasant with a broken wing, or perhaps a fox? I should not mind so much if it were a fox. I hate foxes; they catch young hares when they are asleep and eat them."

"None of these things. I was told that it belonged to a little girl who died. That broke its heart, so that it died also when they shut her up in a box. Therefore it was allowed to accompany her here because it had loved so much. Indeed I saw them together, both very happy, and together they went through those gates."

"If dogs love little girls why don't they love hares, at least as anything likes to be loved, for the dog didn't want to eat the little girl, did it? I see you can't answer me. Now would you like me to tell you my story? Something inside of me is saying that I am to do so if you will listen; also that there is plenty of time, for I am not wanted at present, and when I am I can run to those gates much quicker than you could."

"I should like it very much, Hare. Once a prophet heard an ass speak in order to warn him. But since then, except very, very rarely in dreams, no creature has talked to a man, so far as I know. Perhaps you wish to warn me about something, or others through me, as the ass warned Balaam."

"Who is Balaam? I never heard of Balaam. He wasn't the man who fetches dead pheasants in the donkey-cart, was he? If so, I've seen him make the ass talk—with a thick stick. No? Well, never mind, I daresay I should not understand about him if you told me. Now for my story."

Then the Hare sat itself down, planting its forepaws firmly in front of it, as these animals do when they are on the watch, looked up at me and began to pour the contents of its mind into mine.

I was born, it said, or rather told me by thought transference, in a field of growing corn near to a big wood. At least I suppose I was born there, though the first thing I remember is playing about in the wheat with two other little ones of my own size, a brother and a sister that were born with me. It was at night, for a great, round, shining thing which I now know was the moon, hung in the sky above us. We gambolled together and were very happy, till presently my mother came—I remember how big she looked—and cuffed me with her paw because I had led the others away from the place where she had told us to stop, and given her a great hunt to find us. That is the first thing I remember about my mother. Afterwards she seemed sorry because she had hurt me, and nursed us all three, letting me have the most milk. My mother always loved me the best of us, because I was such a fine leveret, with a pretty grey patch on my left ear. Just as I had finished drinking another hare came who was my father. He was very large, with a glossy coat and big shining eyes that always seemed to see everything, even when it was behind him.

He was frightened about something, and hustled my mother and us little ones out of the wheat-field into the big wood by which it is bordered. As we left the field I saw two tall creatures that afterwards I came to know were men. They were placing wire-netting round the field—you see I understand now what all these things were, although of course I did not at the time. The two ends of the wire netting had nearly come together. There was only a little gap left through which we could run. Another young hare, or it may have been a rabbit, had got entangled in it, and one of the men was beating it to death with a stick. I remember that the sound of its screams made me feel cold down the back, for I had never heard anything like that before, and this was the first that I had seen of pain and death.

The other man saw us slipping through and ran at us with his stick. My mother went first and escaped him. Then came my sister, then I, then my brother. My father was last of all. The man hit with his stick and it came down thud along side of me, just touching my fur. He hit again and broke the foreleg of my brother. Still we all managed to get through into the wood, except my father who was behind.

"There's the old buck!" cried one of the men (I understand what he said now, though at the time it meant nothing to me). "Knock him on the head!"

So leaving us alone they ran at him. But my father was much too quick for them. He rushed back into the corn and afterwards joined us in the wood, for he had seen wire before and knew how to escape it. Still he was terribly frightened and made us keep in the wood till the following evening, not even allowing my mother to go to her form in the rough pasture on its other side and lie up there.

Also we were in trouble because my brother's forepaw was broken. It gave him a great deal of pain, so that he could not rest or sleep. After a while, however, it mended up in a fashion, but he was never able to run as fast as we could, nor did he grow so big. In the end the mother fox killed him, as I shall tell.

My mother asked my father what the men with the sticks were doing—for, you know, many animals can talk to each other in their own way, even if they are of different kinds. He told her that they were protecting the wheat to prevent us from eating it, to which she answered angrily that hares must live somehow, especially when they had young ones to nurse. My father replied that men did not seem to think so, and perhaps they had young ones also. I see now that my father was a philosophic hare. But are you tired of my story?

"Not at all," I answered; "go on, please. It is very interesting to hear things described from the animal's point of view, especially when that animal has grown wise and learned to understand."

"Ah," answered the Hare. "I see what you mean. And it is odd, but I do understand. All has become clear to me. I don't know what happened when I died, but there came a change, and I knew that I who was but a beast always have been and still am a necessary part of everything as much as you are, though more helpless and humble. Yes, I am as ancient and as far-reaching as yourself, but how I began and how I shall end is dark to me. Well, I will go on with my story."

It must have been a moon or so later, after my mother had given up nursing me, that I went to lie out by myself. There was a big house on the hillside overlooking the sea, and near to it were gardens surrounded by a wall. Also outside of this wall was another patch of garden where cabbages grew. I found a way to those cabbages and kept it secret, for I was greedy and wanted them all for myself. I used to creep in at night and eat them, also some flowers with spiky leaves that grew round them which had a very fine flavour. Then after the dawn came I went to a form which I had made under a furze bush on the slope that ran down to the sea, and slept there.

One day I was awakened by something white, hard, and round which rolled gently and stopped still quite close to me. It was not alive, although it had a queer smell, and I wondered why it moved at all. Presently I heard voices and there appeared a little man, and with him somebody who was not a man because it was differently dressed and spoke in a higher voice. I saw that they had sticks in their hands and thought of running away, then that it would be safer to lie quite close. They came up to me and the little man said—

"There's the ball; pick it up, Ella, the lie is too bad."

She, for now I know it was what is called a girl, stooped to obey and saw my back.

"Tom," she said in a whisper, "here's a young hare on its form."

"Get out of the light," he answered, "and I'll kill it," and he lifted the stick he held, which had a twisted iron end.

"No," she said, "catch it alive; I want a hare to be a friend to my rabbit, which has lost all its little ones."

"Lost them? Eaten them, you mean, because you would always go and stare at it," said Tom. "Where's the leveret? Oh! I see. Now, look out!"

A moment later and I was in darkness. Tom had thrown himself upon the top of me and was grabbing at me with his hands. I nearly got away, but as my head poked up under his arm the girl caught hold of it.

"Oh! it's scratching," she cried, as indeed I was with all my might. "Hold it, Tom, hold it!"

"Hold it yourself," said Tom, "my face is full of furze prickles." So she held and presently he helped her, till in the end I was tied up in a pocket-handkerchief and carried I knew not whither. Indeed I was almost mad with fear.

When I came to myself I found that I was within a kind of wire run which smelt foully, as though hundreds of things had lived in it for years. There was a hutch at the end of the run in which sat an enormous she-rabbit, quite as big as my mother, a fierce-looking brute with long yellow teeth. I was afraid of that rabbit and got as far from it as I could. Presently it hopped out and looked at me.

"What are you doing here?" it asked. "Can't you talk? Well, it doesn't matter. If I get hungry I'll eat you! Do you hear that? I'll eat you, as I did all the others," and it showed its big yellow teeth and hopped back into the hutch.

After that Tom and the girl came and gave us plenty of food which the big rabbit ate, for I could touch nothing. For two days they came, and then I think they forgot all about us. I grew very hungry, and at night filled myself with some of the remaining food, such as stale cabbage leaves. By next morning all was gone, and the big rabbit grew hungry also. All that day it hopped about sniffing at me and showing its yellow teeth.

"I shall eat you to-night," it said.

I ran round and round the pen in terror, till at last I found a place where rats had been working under the wire, almost big enough for me to squeeze through, but not quite.

The sun went down and the big she-rabbit came out.

"Now I am going to eat you," it said, "as I ate all the others. I am hungry, very hungry," and it prodded me about with its nose and rolled me over.

At last with a little squeal it drove its big yellow teeth into me behind. Oh! how they hurt! I was near the rat-hole. I rushed at it, scrabbling and wriggling. The big rabbit pounced on me with its fore-feet, trying to hold me, but too late, for I was through, leaving some of my fur behind me. I ran, how I ran! without stopping, till at length I found my mother in the rough pasture by the wood and told her everything.

"Ah!" she said, "that's what comes of greediness and of trying to be too clever. Now, perhaps, you will learn to stop at home."

So I did for a long while.

The summer went by without anything particular happening, except that my brother with the lame foot was eaten by the mother fox. That great red beast was always prowling about, and at night surprised us in a field near the wood where we were feeding on some beautiful turnips. The rest of us got away, but my brother being lame, was not quick enough. The fox caught him, and I heard her sharp white teeth crunch into his bones. The sound made me quite sick, and my mother was very sad afterwards. She complained to my father of the cruelty of foxes, but he, who, as I have said, was a philosopher, answered her almost in her own words.

"Foxes must live, and this one has young to feed, and therefore is always hungry. There are three of them in a hole at the top of the wood," he remarked. "Also our son was lame and would certainly have been caught when the hunting begins."

"What's the hunting?" I asked.

"Never mind," said my father sharply. "No doubt you'll find out in time, that is if you live through the shooting."

"What's the shooting?" I began, but my father cuffed me over the head and I was silent.

I may tell you that my mother soon got over the loss of my brother, for just about that time she had four new little ones, after which neither she nor my father seemed to think any more about us. My sister and I hated those little ones. We two alone remembered my brother, and sometimes wondered whether he was quite gone or would one day come back. The fox, I am glad to say, got caught in a trap. At least I am not glad now—I was glad because, you see, I was so much afraid of her.

THE SHOOTING

I was quite close by one morning when the fox, who was smelling about after me, I suppose because it had liked my brother so much, got caught in the big trap which was covered over artfully with earth and baited with some stuff which stank horribly. I remember it looked very like my own hind-legs. The fox, not being able to find me, went to this filth and tried to eat it.

Then suddenly there was a dreadful fuss. The fox yelped and flew into the air. I saw that a great black thing was fast on its forepaw. How that fox did jump and roll! It was quite wonderful to see her. She looked like a great yellow ball, except for a lot of white marks about the head, which were her teeth. But the trap would not come away, because it was tied to a root with a chain.

At last the fox grew tired and, lying down, began to think, licking its paw as it thought and making a kind of moaning noise. Next it commenced gnawing at the root after trying the chain and finding that its teeth would not go into it. While it was doing this I heard the sound of a man somewhere in the wood. So did the fox, and oh! it looked so frightened. It lay down panting, its tongue hanging out and its ears pressed back against its head, and whisked its big tail from side to side. Then it began to gnaw again, but this time at its own leg. It wanted to bite it off and so get away. I thought this very brave of the fox, and though I hated it because it had eaten my brother and tried to eat me, I felt quite sorry.

It was about half through its leg when the man came. I remember that he had a cat with a little red collar on its neck, and an owl in his hand, both of them dead, for he was Giles, the head-keeper, going round his traps. He was a tall man with sandy whiskers and a rough voice, and he carried a single-barrelled gun under his arm.

You see, now that I am dead I know the use of these things, just as I understand all that was said, though of course at the time it had no meaning for me. Still I find that I have forgotten nothing, not one word from the beginning of my life to the end.

The keeper, who was on his way to the place where he nailed the creatures he did not like by dozens upon poles, looked down and saw the fox. "Oh! my beauty," he said, "so I have got you at last. Don't you think yourself clever trying to bite off that leg. You'd have done it too, only I came along just in time. Well, good night, old girl, you won't have no more of my pheasants."

Then he lifted the gun. There was a most dreadful noise and the fox rolled over and lay still.

"There you are, all neat and tidy, my dear," said the keeper. "Now I must just tuck you away in the hollow tree before old Grampus sneaks round and sees you, for if he should it will be almost as much as my place is worth."

Next he set his foot on the trap and, opening it, took hold of the fox by the fore-legs to carry it off. The cat and the owl he stuffed away into a great pocket in his coat.

"Jemima! don't you wholly stink," he said, then gave a most awful yell.

The fox wasn't quite dead after all, it was only shamming dead. At any rate it got Giles' hand in its mouth and made its teeth meet through the flesh.

Now the keeper began to jump about just as the fox had done when it set its paw in the trap, shouting and saying all sorts of things that somehow I don't think I ought to repeat here. Round and round he went with the fox hanging to his hand, like hares do when they dance together, for he couldn't get it off anyhow. At last he tumbled down into a pool of mud and water, and when he got up again all wet through I saw that the fox was really dead. But it had died biting, and now I know that this pleased it very much.

It was just then that the man whom the keeper had called Grampus came up. He was a big, fat man with a very red face, who made a kind of blowing noise when he walked fast. I know now that he was the lord of all the other men about that place, that he lived in the house which looked over the sea, and that the boy and girl who put me in with the yellow-toothed rabbit were his children. He was what the farmers called "a first-rate all-round sportsman," which means, my friend—but what is your name?

"Oh! Mahatma," I answered at hazard.

"Which means, my friend Mahatma, that he spent most of the year in killing the lower animals such as me. Yes, he spent quite eight months out of the twelve in killing us one way and another, for when there was no more killing to be done in his own country, he would travel to others and kill there. He would even kill pigeons from a trap, or young rooks just out of their nests, or rats in a stack, or sparrows among ivy, rather than not kill anything. I've heard Giles say so to the under-keeper and call him 'a regular slaughterer' and 'a true-blood Englishman.'

"Yet, my friend Mahatma, I say in the light of the truth which has come to me, that according to his knowledge Grampus was a good man. Thus, what little time he had to spare from sport he passed in helping his brother men by sending them to prison. Although of course he never worked or earned anything, he was very rich, because money flowed to him from other people who had been very rich, but who at last were forced to travel this Road and could not bring it with them. If they could have brought it, I am sure that Grampus would never have got any. However, he did get it, and he aided a great many people with that part of it which he found he could not spend upon himself. He was a very good man, only he liked killing us lower creatures, whom he bred up with his money to be killed.

"Go on with your story, Hare," I said; "when I see this Red-faced Man I will judge of him for myself. Probably you are prejudiced about him."

"I daresay I am," answered the Hare, rubbing its nose; "but please observe that I am not speaking unkindly of Grampus, although before I have done you may think that I might have reason to do so. However, you will be able to form your own opinion when he comes here, which I am sure he does not mean to do for many, many years. The world is much too comfortable for him. He does not wish to leave it."

"Still he may be obliged to do so, Hare."

"Oh! no, people like that are never obliged to do anything they do not like. It is only poor things such as you and I, Mahatma, which must suffer. I can see that you have had a great deal to bear, and so have I, for we were born to suffering as the Red-faced Man was born to happiness."

"Go on with your story, Hare," I repeated. "You are becoming metaphysical and therefore dull. The time is short and I want to hear what happened."

"Quite so, Mahatma. Well, Grampus came up breathing very heavily and looking very red in the face. He held his hat in one hand and a large crooked stick in the other, and even the top of his head, on which no hair grew, was red, for he had been running.

"What the deuce is the matter?" he puffed. "Oh! it is you, Giles, is it? What are you doing, sir, looking like that, all covered with blood and mud? Has a poacher shot you, or what?"

"No, Squire," answered Giles humbly, touching his hat. "I have shot a poacher, that's all, and it has given me what for," and he lifted the body of the fox from the water.

"A fox," said Grampus, "a fox! Do you mean to say, Giles, that you have dared to shoot a fox, and a vixen with a litter too? How often have I told you that, although I keep harriers and not fox-hounds, you are never to touch a fox. You will get me into trouble with all my neighbours. I give you a month's notice. You will leave on this day month."

"Very well, Squire," said Giles, "I'll leave, and I hope you'll find some one to serve you better. Meanwhile I didn't shoot the dratted fox. At least I only shot her after she'd gone and got herself into a trap which I had set for that there Rectory dog what you told me to make off with on the quiet, so that the young lady might never know what become of it and cry and make a fuss as she did about the last. Then seeing that she was finished, with her leg half chewed off, I shot her, or rather I didn't shoot her as well as I should, for the beggar gave a twist as I fired, and now she's bit me right through the hand. I only hopes you won't have to pay my widow for it, Squire, under the Act, as foxes' bites is uncommon poisonous, especially when they've been a-eating of rotten rabbit."

"Dear me!" said the Red-faced Man softening, "dear me, the beast does seem to have bitten you very badly. You must go and be cauterised with a red-hot iron. It is painful but the best thing to do. Meanwhile, suck it, Giles, suck it! I daresay that will draw out the poison, and if it doesn't, thank my stars! I am insured. Look here, a minute or two can make no difference, for if you are poisoned, you are poisoned. Where can we put this brute? I wouldn't have it seen for ten pounds."

"There's an old pollard, Squire, about five yards away down near the fence, which is hollow and handy," said Giles.

"Quite so," he answered, "I know it well. Do you bring the—dog, Giles. Remember, it was a dog, not a fox."

Then they went to the pollard, and as Giles's hand was hurt the Red-faced Man climbed up it, though Giles tried to prevent him.

"Now then, Giles," he said, "give me the fox—I mean the dog, and I will drop it down. Great Heavens! how this tree stinks. Has there been an earth here?"

"Not as I knows of, Squire," said Giles sullenly.

Grampus stretched his hand down into the hollow of the pollard and dragged up a rotting fox by its tail.

"Giles," he said, "you have been killing more foxes and hiding them in this tree. Giles, I dismiss you at once and without a month's wages."

"All right, sir," said Giles, "I'll go, and I prays you'll find some one what will keep your hares which you must have, and your pheasants which you must have, and your partridges which you must have, without killing these varmints of foxes what eats the lot."

The Red-faced Man descended from the tree holding his nose and looked at Giles. Giles sucked his bleeding hand and looked at him.

"Foxes are very destructive animals," said the Red-faced Man to Giles, "especially when one shoots and keeps harriers."

"They are that, sir," said Giles to the Red-faced Man, "as only those know what has to do with them."

"Put the other in, Giles," said the Red-faced man, "and when you have time, throw some soil on to the top of the lot. This place smells horrible. And look you here, Giles," he added in a voice of thunder, "if ever I find you killing a fox upon this property, you will be dismissed at once, as I have often told you before. Do you understand?"

"Yes, Squire, I understand," answered Giles, "and I'll see to the burying of them this same afternoon, if the pain in my hand will suffer it."

"Very well," said the Red-faced Man, "that's done with—except the cubs. As you have killed the vixen you had better stink the cubs out of the earth. I daresay they are old enough to look after themselves— at any rate I hope so. And now, Giles, we must shoot some of these hares when we begin on the partridges next week. There are too many of them, the tenants are complaining, ungrateful beggars as they are, seeing that I keep them for their sport."

At this point I thought that I had heard enough, and slipped away when their backs were turned. For, friend Mahatma, I had just seen a fox shot, and now I knew what shooting meant.

About a week later I knew better still. It came about thus. By that time the turnips I have mentioned, those that grew in the big field, had swelled into fine, large bulbs with leafy tops. We used to eat them at nights, and in the daytime to lie up among them in our snug forms. You know, Mahatma, don't you, that a form is a little hollow which a hare makes in the ground just to fit itself? No hare likes to sleep in another hare's form. Do you understand?"

"Yes," I answered, "I understand. It would be like a man wearing another man's boots."

"I don't know anything about boots Mahatma, except that they are hard things with iron on them which kick one out of one's form if one sits too close. Once that happened to me. Well, my form was under a particularly fine turnip that had some dead leaves beneath the green ones. I chose it because, like the brown earth, they just matched the colour of my back. I was sleeping there quite soundly when my sister came and woke me.

"There are men in the field," she said, her eyes nearly starting out of her head with fear, for she was always very timid.

"I'm off."

"Are you?" I answered. "Well, I think I shall stop here where I shan't be noticed. If we begin jumping over those turnips they will see us."

"We might run down the rows, keeping our ears close to our backs," she remarked.

"No," I said, "there are too many bare patches."

At this moment a gun went 'bang' some way off; and my sister, like a wise hare, scuttled away at full speed for the wood. But I only made myself smaller than usual and lay watching and listening.

There was a good deal to see and hear; for instance, a covey of partridges, troublesome birds that come scratching and fidgeting about when one wants to sleep, were running to and fro in a great state of concern.

"They are after us," said the old cock.

"I remember the same thing last year. Come on, do."

"How can I with all these young ones to look after?" answered the hen. "Why, if once they are scattered I shall never find them again."

"Just as you like, you know best," said the cock. "Goodbye," and away he flew, while his wife and the rest ran to a little distance, scattered and squatted.

Presently, looking back over my shoulders without turning my head, as a hare can, I saw a line of men walking towards me. There was the Red-faced Man whom Giles called Grampus behind his back and Squire to his face. There was Giles himself, with his hurt hand tied up, holding a kind of stick with a slit in it from which hung a lot of dead partridges whose necks were in the slit. One of them was not dead or had come to life again, for it flapped in the stick trying to fly away. He held these in the hand that was tied up, and in the other, oh, horror! was a dead hare bleeding from its nose. It looked uncommonly like my mother, but whether it were or no I couldn't be quite sure. At least from that day neither my sister nor I ever saw her again. I suppose you haven't met her coming up this big white Road, have you, Mahatma?

"No, no," I answered impatiently, "I have already told you that you are the first hare I have ever seen upon the Road. Please get on with your story, or the Lights will change and the Gates be opened before I hear its end."

Just when I saw her I was thinking of running away, but the sight terrified me so much that I could not stir. You see, Mahatma, I really loved my mother as much as a hare can love anything, which is a good deal.

Well, beyond Giles was, who do you think? That dreadful boy, Tom, with a gun in his hand too. Did I say that they all had guns, except Giles and some beater men, only that Tom's was single-barrelled? Then there were others whom I need not describe, stretching to left and right, and worst of all, perhaps, there was Giles's great black dog, a silly-looking beast which always seemed to have its mouth open and its tongue hanging out, and to be wagging a big tail like the fox's, only black and more ragged.

As I watched, up got the old hen partridge and one of her young ones and flew towards me. The Red-faced Man lifted his gun and fired, once, twice, and down came first the mother partridge and then the young one. I forgot to say that Tom fired too at the old partridge, which fell dead quite close to me, leaving a lot of feathers floating in the air. As it fell Tom screeched out—

"I killed that, father."

This made the Red-faced Man very angry.

"You young scoundrel," he said, "how often have I told you not to shoot at my birds under my nose? No sportsman shoots at another man's birds, and as for killing it, you were yards under the thing. If you do it again I will send you home."

"Sorry, father," said Tom, adding in a low voice with a snigger, "I did kill it after all. Dad thinks no one can hit a partridge except himself."

Just then up jumped my father near to Giles, and came leaping in front of the Red-faced Man about twenty yards away from him.

"Mark hare!" shouted Giles, and Grampus, who was still glowering at Tom and had not quite finished pushing the cartridges into his gun, shut it up in a hurry and fired first one barrel and then the other. But my father, who was very cunning, jumped into the air at the first shot and ducked at the second, so that he was missed; at least I suppose that is why he was missed.

Giles grinned and the Red-faced Man said, "Damn!" What does 'damn' mean, Mahatma? It was a very favourite word with the Red-faced Man, but even now I can't quite understand it."

"Nor can I," I answered. "Go on."

"Well, my poor father next ran in front of Tom, who shot too and hit him in the hind legs so that he rolled over and over in the turnips, kicking and screaming. Have you ever heard a hare scream, Mahatma?"

"Yes, yes, it makes a horrid noise like a baby."

"Wiped your eye that time, Dad," cried Tom in an exultant voice.

"I don't know about wiping my eye," answered his father, turning quite purple with rage, "but I wish you would be good enough, Thomas, not to shoot my hares behind, so that they make that beastly row which upsets me" (I think that the Red-faced Man was really kind at the bottom) "and spoils them for the market. If you can't hit a hare in front, miss it like a gentleman."

"As you do, Dad," said Tom, sniggering again. "All right, I'll try."

"Giles," roared Grampus, pretending not to hear, "send your dog and fetch that hare. I can't bear its screeching."

So that great black dog rushed forward and caught my poor father in its big mouth, although he tried to drag himself away on his front paws, and after that I shut my eyes.

Then a lot of partridges got up and there was any amount of banging, though most of them were missed. This made the Red-faced Man angrier than ever. He took off his hat and waved it, bellowing—

"Call back that brute of a dog of yours, Giles. Call it back at once or I'll shoot it."

So Giles called, "Nigger. Come you 'ere, Nigger! Nigg, Nigg, Nigg!"

But Nigger rushed about putting up partridges all over the place while Grampus stamped and shouted and every one missed everything, till at last Tom sat down on the turnips and roared with laughter.

At length, after Giles had beaten Nigger till he broke a stick over him, making him howl terribly, order was restored, and the line having reformed, began to march down on me. For, Mahatma, I was so frightened by what had happened to my father, and I think my mother, that I didn't remember what he, I mean my dead father, had told me, always to run away when there is a chance, as poor hares can only protect themselves by flight.

So as I had lost the chance I thought that I would just sit tight, hoping that they would not see me. Nor indeed would they if it hadn't been for that horrible Tom.

During the confusion the mother partridge which the Red-faced Man had shot had been forgotten by everybody except Tom. Tom, you see, was certain that he had shot it himself, being a very obstinate boy, and was determined to retrieve it as his own.

Now that partridge had fallen within a yard of me, with its beak and claws pointing to the sky, and when the line had passed where we lay Tom lagged behind to look for it. He did not find it then, whether he ever found it afterwards I am sure I don't know. But he found me.

"By Jove! here's a hare," he said, and made a grab at me just as he had done in the furze bush.

Well, I went. Tom shot when I wasn't more than four yards from him, and the whole charge passed like a bullet between my hind legs and struck the ground under my stomach, sending up such a shower of earth and stones that I was knocked right over.

"I've hit it!" yelled Tom, as he crammed another cartridge into his single-barrelled gun.

By the time that it was loaded I was quite thirty yards away and going like the wind. Tom lifted the gun.

"Don't shoot!" roared the Red-faced Man.

"Mind that there boy!" bellowed Giles.

I was running down between two rows of turnips and presently butted into a lad who was bending over, I suppose to pick up a partridge. At any rate his tail—"do you call it his tail, Mahatma?"

"That will do," I answered.

"Well, his tail was towards me; it looked very round and shiny. The shot from Tom's gun hit it everywhere. I wish they had all gone into it, but as he was so far away the charge scattered and six of the bullets struck me. Oh! they did hurt. Put your hand on my back, Mahatma, and you will feel the six lumps they made beneath the grey tufts of hair that grew over them, for they are still there."

Forgetting that we were on the Road, I stretched out my hand; but, of course, it went quite through the hare, although I could see the six little grey tufts clearly enough.

"You are foolish, Hare; you don't remember that your body is not here but somewhere else."

"Quite true, Mahatma. If it were here I could not be talking to you, could I? As a matter of fact, I have no body now. It is—oh, never mind where. Still, you can see the grey tufts, can't you? Well, I only hope that those shot hurt that fat boy half as much as they did me. No, I don't mean that I hope it now, I used to hope it."

My goodness! didn't he screech, much worse than my father when his legs were broken. And didn't everybody else roar and shout, and didn't I dance? Off I went right over the fat boy, who had tumbled down, up to the end of the field, then so bewildered was I with shock and the burning pain, back again quite close to them.

But now nobody shot at me because they all thought the boy was killed and were gathered round him looking very solemn. Only I saw that the Red-faced Man had Tom by the neck and was kicking him hard.

After that I saw no more, for I ran five miles before I stopped, and at last lay down in a little swamp near the seashore to which my mother had once taken me. My back was burning like fire, and I tried to cool it in the soft slush.

THE COURSING

Quite a moon went by before I recovered from Tom's shot. At first I thought that I was going to die, for, although luckily none of my bones were broken, the pain in my back was dreadful. When I tried to ease the agony by rubbing against roots it only became worse, for the fur fell off, leaving sores upon which flies settled. I could scarcely eat or sleep, and grew so thin that the bones nearly poked through my pelt. Indeed I wanted very much to die, but could not. On the contrary, by degrees I recovered, till at last I was quite strong again and like other hares, except for the six little grey tufts upon my back and one hole through my right ear.

Now all this while I had lived in the swamp near the sea, but when my strength returned I thought of my old home, to which something seemed to draw me. Also there were no turnips near the swamp, and as the winter came on I found very little to eat there. So one day, or rather one night, I travelled back home.

As it happened the first hare that I met near the big wood was my sister. She was very glad to see me, although she had forgotten how we came to part, and when I spoke of our father and mother these did not seem to interest her. Still from that time forward we lived together more or less till her end came.

One day—this was after we had made our home in the big wood, as hares often do in winter—there was a great disturbance. When we tried to go out to feed at daylight we found little fires burning everywhere, and near to them boys who beat themselves and shouted. So we went back into the wood, where the pheasants were running to and fro in a great state of mind.

Some hours later, when the sun was quite high, men began to march about and scores of shots were fired a long way off, also a wounded cock-pheasant fell near to us and fluttered away, making a queer noise in its throat. It looked very funny stumbling along on one leg with its beak gaping and two of the long feathers in its tail broken.

"I know what this is," I said to my sister. "Let's be gone before they shoot us. I've had enough of being shot."

So off we went, rushing past a boy by his fire, who yelled and threw a stick at us. But as it happened, on the borders of the property of the Red-faced Man there were poachers who knew that hares would come out of the wood on this day of the shooting and had made ready for us by setting wire nooses in the gaps of the hedges through which we ran. I got my foot into one of these but managed to shake it off. My sister was not so lucky, for her head went into another of them. She kicked and tore, but the more she struggled the tighter drew the noose.

I watched her for a little while until one of the poachers ran up with a stick.

Then I went away, as I could not bear to see her beaten to death, and that was the end of my sister. So now I was the only one left alive of our family, except perhaps some younger brothers whom I did not know, though I think it was one of these that afterwards I saw shot quite dead by Giles. He went over and over and lay as still as though he had never moved in all his life. Death seems a very wonderful thing, Mahatma, but I won't ask you what it is because I perceive that you can't answer.

After this nothing happened to me for a long while. Indeed I had the best time of my life and grew very strong and big, yes, the strongest and biggest hare of any that I ever saw, also the swiftest of foot. Twice I was chased by dogs; once by Giles's black beast, Nigger, and once by that of a shepherd. Finding that I could run right away from them without exerting myself at all, I grew to despise dogs. Ah! little did I know then that there are many different breeds of these animals.

One day in mid-winter, as the weather was very mild and open, I was lying on the rough grass field that I have spoken of which borders a flat stretch of moorland. On this moorland in summer grew tall ferns, but now these had died and been broken down by the wind. Suddenly I woke up from my sleep to see a number of men walking and riding towards me.

They were tenants and others who, although the real coursing season had not yet begun in our neighbourhood, had been asked by Grampus to come to try their greyhounds upon his land. Those of them who walked for the most part held two long, lean dogs on a string, while one or two carried dead hares. They were dreadful-looking hares that seemed to have been bitten all over; at least their coats were wet and broken. I shivered at the sight of them, feeling sure that I was going to be put to some new kind of torture.

Besides the men on foot were those on horseback, among whom I recognised the Red-faced Man and my enemy, the dreadful Tom. Most of the others were people called farmers, who seemed very happy and excited and from time to time drank something out of little bottles which they passed to each other. Giles was not there. Now I know that this was because he hated coursing, which killed down hares. Hares, he thought, out to be shot, not coursed.

Whilst I watched, wondering what to do, there was a shout of "There she goes!" and all the long dogs began to pull at their strings. Off the necks of two of them the collars seemed to fall, and away they leapt pursuing a hare. The men on the horses galloped after them, but the men on foot remained where they were.

Now I was afraid to get up and run lest they should loose the other dogs on me, so I lay still, till presently I saw the hare coming back towards me, followed by the two dogs whose noses almost touched its tail. It was exhausted and tried to twist and spring away to the right. But as it did so one of the dogs caught it in its mouth and bit it till it died.

"That was a rotten hare," said Tom, who cantered up just then, "it gave no course at all."

"Yes," puffed Grampus. "Hope the next one will show better sport."

"Hope so too," answered Tom, "especially as it is Jack and Jill's turn to be slipped, and they are the best greyhounds for twenty miles round."

Then the Red-faced Man gave some orders and Jack and Jill were brought forward by the man whose business it was to slip the dogs. One of them was black and one yellow; I think Jack was the black one—a dreadful, sneaking-looking beast with a white tip to its tail, which ended in a sort of curl.

"Forward now," said Grampus, "and go slow. There's sure to be another puss or two in this rough grass."

Next second I was up and away, and before you could count twelve Jack and Jill were after me. I saw them standing on their hind legs straining at the cord. Then the collars fell from them and they leapt forward like the light. My thought was to get back to the wood, which was about a minute's run behind me, but I did not dare to turn and head for it because of the long line of people through which I must pass if I tried to do so. So I ran straight for the moorland, hoping to turn there and reach the wood on its other side, although this meant a long journey.

For a while all went well with me, and having a good start I began to hope that I should outrun these beasts, as I had the shepherd's dog and the retriever. But I did not know Jack and Jill. Just as I reached the borders of the moor I heard the patter of their feet behind me, and looking back saw them coming up, about as far away as I was from Tom when he shot me.

They were running quite close together and behind them galloped the judge and other men. There was a fence here and I bolted through a hole in it. The greyhounds jumped over and for a moment lost sight of me, for I had turned and run down near the side of the fence. But Tom, who had come through a gap, saw me and waved his arm shouting, and next instant Jack and Jill saw me too.

Then as the going was rough by the fence I took to the open moor, always trying, however, to work round to the left in the hope that I might win the shelter of the wood.

On we went like the wind, and now Jack and Jill were quite close behind me, though before they got there I had managed to circle so that at last my head pointed to the wood, which was more than half a mile away. Their speed was greater than mine, and I knew that I must soon be caught.

At last they were not more than two yards behind, and for the first time I twisted so that they overshot me, which gave me another start. Three times they came up and three times I wrenched or twisted. The wood was not so far away now, but I was almost spent.

What was I to do! What was I to do! I saw a clump of furze to the left, a big clump and thick, and remembered that there was a hare's run through it. I reached it just as Jill was on the top of me, and once more they lost sight of me for a while as they ran round the clump staring and jumping. When they saw me again on the further side I was thirty yards ahead of them and the wood was perhaps two hundred and fifty yards away. But now I could only run more slowly, for my heart seemed to be bursting, though luckily Jack and Jill were getting tired also. Still they soon came up, and now I must twist every few yards, or be caught in their jaws.

I can't tell you what I felt, Mahatma, and until you have been hunted by greyhounds you will never know. It was horrible. Yet I managed to twist and jump so that always Jack and Jill just missed me. The farmers on the horses laughed to see my desperate leaps and wrenches.

But Tom did worse than laugh. Noting that I was getting quite near the wood, he rode between me and it, trying to turn me into the open, for he wished to see me killed.

"Don't do that! It isn't sportsmanlike," shouted the Red-faced Man. "Give the poor beast a chance."

I don't know whether he obeyed or not, as just then I made my last double, and felt Jill's teeth cut through the fur of my scut and heard them snap. I had dodged Jill, but Jack was right on to me and the wood still twenty yards away.

I could not twist any more, it was just which of us could get there first. I gathered all my remaining strength, for I was mad, mad with terror, and bounded forward.

After me came Jack, I felt his hot breath on my flank. I jumped the ditch, yes, I found power to jump that ditch where there was a rabbit run just by the trunk of a young oak. Jack jumped after me; we must both have been in the air at the same time. But I got through the rabbit run, whereas Jack hit his sharp nose against the trunk of the tree and broke his neck. Yes, he fell dead into the ditch.

I crawled on a few yards to a thick clump and squatted down, for I could not stir another inch. So it came about that I heard them all talking on the other side.

One of them said I was the finest hare he had ever coursed. Others, who had dragged Jack out of the ditch, lamented his death, especially the owner, who vowed that he was worth £50 and abused Tom. Tom, he said, had caused him to be killed—I don't know how, but I suppose because he had ridden forward and tried to turn me. The Red-faced Man also scolded Tom. Then he added—

"Well, I am glad she got off, for she'll give us a good run with the harriers one day. I shall always know that hare again by the white marks on its back; also it is the biggest I have seen for a long while. Come on, my friends, the dog is dead and there's an end of it. At least we have had a good morning's sport, so let's go to the Hall and get some lunch."

The Hare paused for a little, then looked up at me in its comical fashion and asked—

"Did you ever course hares, Mahatma?"

"Not I, thank goodness," I answered.

"Well, what do you think of coursing?"

"I would rather not say," I replied.

"Then I will," said the Hare, with conviction. "I think it horrible."

"Yes, but, Hare, you do not remember the pleasure this sport gives to the men and the dogs; you look at it from an entirely selfish point of view."

"And so would you, Mahatma, if you had felt Jack's hot breath on your back and Jill's teeth in your tail."

THE HUNTING

The Hare sat silent for a time, while I employed myself in watching certain shadows stream past us on the Great White Road. Among them was that of a politician whom I had much admired upon the earth. In this land of Truth I was grieved to observe certain characteristics about him which I had never before suspected. It seemed to me, alas! that in his mundane career he had not been so entirely influenced by a single-hearted desire for the welfare of our country as he had proclaimed and I had believed. I gathered even that his own interests had sometimes inspired his policy.

He went by, leaving, so far as I was concerned, a somewhat painful impression from which I sought relief in the company of the open-souled Hare.

"Well," I said, "I suppose that you died of exhaustion after your coursing experience, and came on here."

"Died of exhaustion, Mahatma, not a bit of it! In three days I was as well as ever, only much more cunning than I had been before. In the night I fed in the fields upon whatever I could get, but in the daytime I always lay up in woods. This I did because I found out the shooting was over, and I knew that greyhounds, which run by sight, would never come into woods."

The weeks went by and the days began to lengthen. Pretty yellow flowers that I had not seen before appeared in the woods, and I ate plenty of them; they have a nice flavour. Then I met another hare and loved her, because she reminded me of my sister. We used to play about together and were very happy. "I wonder what she will do now that I am gone."

"Console herself with somebody else," I suggested sarcastically.

"No, she won't do that, Mahatma, because the hounds 'chopped' her just outside the Round Plantation. I mean they caught and ate her. You think that I am contradicting myself, but I am not. I mean I wonder what she will do without me in whatever world she has reached, for I don't see her here." Well, I went to the little Round Plantation because I found that Giles seldom came there and I thought it would be safer, but as it proved I made a great mistake. One day there appeared the Red-faced Man and Tom and the girl, Ella, and a lot of other people mounted on horses, some of them dressed in green coats with ridiculous-looking caps on their heads.

Also with them were I don't know how many spotted dogs whose tails curled over their backs, not like greyhounds whose tails curl between their legs. Outside of the Plantation those dogs caught and ate my future wife, as I have said. It was her own fault, for I had warned her not to go there, but she was a very self-willed character. As it was she never even gave them a run, for they were all round her in a minute.

Then they made a kind of cartwheel; their heads were in the centre of this cartwheel and their tails pointed out. In its exact middle was my future wife.

When the wheel broke up there was nothing of her left except her scut, which lay upon the ground.

I had seen so many of such things that I was not so much shocked as you might suppose. After all a fine hare like myself could always get another wife, and as I have told you she was very self-willed.

So I lay still, thinking that those men and dogs would go away.

But what do you think Mahatma? Just as they were going the boy Tom called out—

"I say, Dad, I think we might as well knock through the Round Plantation. Giles tells me that the old speckle-backed buck lies up here."

"Does he?" said Grampus. "Well, if so, that's the hare I want to see, for I know he'd give us a good run. Here, Jerry" (Jerry was the huntsman), "just put the hounds into that place."

So Jerry put the hounds in, making dreadful noises to encourage them, and of course I came out, as I did not wish to share the fate of my future wife.

"That's him!" screeched Tom. "Look at the grey marks on his back."

"Yes, that's he right enough," shouted the Red-faced Man. "Lay them on, Jerry, lay them on; we're in for a rattling run now, I'll warrant."

So they were laid on and I went away as hard as my legs would carry me. Very soon I found that I had left all those curly-tailed dogs a long way behind.

"Ah!" I said to myself proudly, "these beasts are not greyhounds; they are like Giles's retriever and the sheep dog. They'll never see me again." So I looped along saving my breath and heading for a wood which was quite five miles off that I had once visited from the Marsh on the sea-shore where I lay sick, for I was sure they would never follow me there.

You can imagine, then, Mahatma, how surprised I was when I drew near that wood to hear a hideous noise of dogs all barking together behind me, and on looking back, to see those spotted brutes, with their tongues hanging out, coming along quite close to each other and not more than a quarter of a mile away.

Moreover they were coming after me. I was sure of that, for the first of them kept setting its nose to the ground just where I had run, and then lifting up its head to bay. Yes, they were coming on my scent. They could smell me as Giles's curly dog smells the wounded partridges. My heart sank at the thought, but presently I remembered that the wood was quite close, and that there I should certainly give them the slip.

So I went on quite cheerfully, not even running as fast as I could. But fortune was against me, as everything has always been, for I never found a friend. I ran along the side of a hedgerow which went quite up to the wood, not knowing that at the end of it three men were engaged in cutting down an oak tree. You see, Mahatma, they had caught sight of the hunt and stopped from their work, so that I did not hear the sound of their axes upon the tree. Nor, as my head was so near the ground, did I see them until I was right on to them, at which moment also they saw me.

"Here she is!" yelled one of them. "Keep her out of covert or they'll lose her," and he threw out his arms and began to jump about, as did the other two.

I pulled up short within three or four yards of them. Behind were the dogs and the people galloping upon horses and in front were the three men. What was I to do? Now I had stopped exactly in a gateway, for a lane ran alongside the wood. After a moment's pause I bolted through the gateway, thinking that I would get into the wood beyond. But one of the men, who of course wanted to see me killed, was too quick for me and there headed me again.

Then I lost my senses. Instead of running on past him and leaping into the wood, I swung right round and rushed back, still clinging to the hedgerow. Indeed as I went down one side of it the hounds and the hunters came up on the other, so that there were only a few sticks between us, though fortunately the wind was blowing from them to me. Fearing lest they should see me I jumped into the ditch and ran for quite two hundred yards through the mud and water that was gathered there. Then I had to come out of it again as it ended but here was a fall in the ground, so still I was not seen.

Meanwhile the hunt had reached the three men and I heard them all talking together. The end of it was that the men explained which way I had gone, and once more the hounds were laid on to me. In a minute they got to where I had entered the ditch, and there grew confused because my footmarks did not smell in the water. For quite a long time they looked about till at length, taking a wide cast, the hounds found my smell again at the end of the ditch.

During this check I was making the best of my way back towards my own home; indeed had it not been for it I should have been caught and torn to pieces much sooner than I was. Thus it happened that I had covered quite three miles before once more I heard those hounds baying behind me. This was just as I got on to the moorland, at that edge of it which is about another three miles from the great house called the Hall, which stands on the top of a cliff that slopes down to the beach and the sea.

I had thought of making for the other wood, that in which I had saved myself from the greyhounds when the beast Jack broke its neck against the tree, but it was too far off, and the ground was so open that I did not dare to try.

So I went straight on, heading towards the cliff. Another mile and they viewed me, for I heard Tom yell with delight as he stood up in his stirrups on the black cob he was riding and waved his cap. Jerry the huntsman also stood up in his stirrups and waved his cap, and the last awful hunt began.

I ran—oh! how I ran. Once when they were nearly on me I managed to check them for a minute in a hollow by getting among some sheep. But they soon found me again, and came after me at full tear not more than a hundred yards behind. In front of me I saw something that looked like walls and bounded towards them with my last strength. My heart was bursting, my eyes and mouth seemed to be full of blood, but the terror of being torn to pieces still gave me power to rush on almost as quickly as though I had just been put off my form. For as I have told you, Mahatma, I am, or rather was, a very strong and swift hare.

I reached the walls; there was an open doorway in them through which I fled, to find myself in a big garden. Two gardeners saw me and shouted loudly. I flew on through some other doors, through a yard, and into a passage where I met a woman carrying a pail, who shrieked and fell on to her back. I jumped over her and got into a big room, where was a long table covered with white on which were all sorts of things that I suppose men eat. Out of that room I went into yet another, where a fat woman with a hooked nose was seated holding something white in front of her. I bolted under the thing on which she was seated and lay there. She saw me come and began to shriek also, and presently a most terrible noise arose outside.

All the spotted dogs were in the house, baying and barking, and everybody was yelling. Then for a minute the dogs stopped their clamour, and I heard a great clatter of things breaking and of teeth crunching and of the Red-faced Man shouting—

"Those cursed brutes are eating the hunt lunch. Get them out, Jerry, you idiot! Get them out! Great heavens! what's the matter with her Ladyship? Is any one murdering her?"

I suppose that they couldn't get them out, or at least when they did they all came into the other room where I was under the seat on which the fat woman was now standing.

"What is it, mother?" I heard Tom say.

"An animal!" she screamed. "An animal under the sofa!"

"All right," he said, "that's only the hare. Here, hounds, out with her, hounds!"

The dogs rushed about, some of them with great lumps of food still in their mouths. But they were confused, and all went into the wrong places. Everything began to fall with dreadful crashes, the fat woman shrieked piercingly, and her shriek was—

"China! Oh! my china-a. John, you wretch! Help! Help! Help!"

To which the Red-faced Man roared in answer—

"Don't be an infernal fool, Eliza-a. I say, don't be such an infernal fool."

Also there were lots of other noises that I cannot remember, except one which a dog made.

This silly dog had thrust its head up the hole over a fire such as the stops make outside the coverts when men are going to shoot, either to hide something or to look for me there. When it came down again because the Red-faced Man kicked it, the dog put its paws into the fire and pulled it all out over the floor. Also it howled very beautifully. Just then another hound, that one which generally led the pack, began to sniff about near me and finally poked its nose under the stuff which hid me.

It jumped back and bayed, whereon I jumped out the other side. Tom made a rush at me and knocked the fat woman off the thing she was standing on, so that she fell among the dogs, which covered her up and began to sniff her all over. Flying from Tom I found myself in front of something filmy, beyond which I saw grass. It looked suspicious, but as nothing in the world could be so bad as Tom, no, not even his dogs, I jumped at it.

There was a crash and a sharp point cut my nose, but I was out upon the grass. Then there were twenty other crashes, and all the hounds were out too, for Tom had cheered them on. I ran to the edge of the lawn and saw a steep slope leading to the sands and the sea. Now I knew what the sea was, for after Tom had shot me in the back I lived by it for a long while, and once swam across a little creek to get to my form, from which it cut me off.

While I ran down that slope fast as my aching legs would carry me, I made up my mind that I would swim out into the sea and drown there, since it is better to drown than to be torn to pieces. "But why are you laughing, friend Mahatma."

"I am not laughing," I said. "In this state, without a body, I have nothing to laugh with. Still you are right, for you see that I should be laughing if I could. Your story of the stout lady and the dogs and the china is very amusing."

"Perhaps, friend, but it did not amuse me. Nothing is amusing when one is going to be eaten alive."

"Of course it isn't," I answered. "Please forgive me and go on."

"Well, I tumbled down that cliff, followed by some of the dogs and Tom and the girl Ella and the huntsman Jerry on foot, and dragged myself across the sands till I came to the lip of the sea."

Just here there was a boat and by it stood Giles the keeper. He had come there to get out of the way of the hunting, which he hated as much as he did the coursing. The sight of him settled me—into the sea I went. The dogs wanted to follow me, but Jerry called and whipped them off.

"I won't have them caught in the current and drowned," he said. "Let the flea-bitten old devil go, she's brought trouble enough already."

"Help me shove off the boat, Giles," shouted Tom. "She shan't beat us; we must have her for the hounds. Come on, Ella."

"Best leave her alone, Master Tom," said Giles. "I think she's an unlucky one, that I do."

Still the end of it was that he helped to float the little boat and got into it with Tom and Ella.

Just after they had pushed off I saw a man running down the steps on the cliff waving his arms while he called out something. But of him they took no heed. I do not think they noticed him. As for me, I swam on.

I could not go very fast because I was so dreadfully tired; also I did not like swimming, and the cold waves broke over my head, making the cut in my nose smart and filling my eyes with something that stung them. I could not see far either, nor did I know where I was going. I knew nothing except I was about to die, and that soon everything would be at an end; men, dogs—everything, yes, even Tom. I wanted things to come to an end. I had suffered so dreadfully, life was so horrible, I was so very tired. I felt that it was better to die and have done.

So I swam on a long way and began to forget things; indeed I thought that I was playing in the big turnip field with my mother and sister. But just as I was sinking exhausted a hand shot down into the water and caught me by the ears, although from below the fingers looked as though they were bending away from me. I saw it coming and tried to sink more quickly, but could not.

"I've got her," said the voice of Tom gleefully. "My! isn't she a beauty? Over nine pounds if she is an ounce. Only just in time, though," he went on, "for, look! she's drowning; her head wobbles as though she were sea-sick. Buck up, pussie, buck up! You mustn't cheat the hounds at last, you know. It wouldn't be sportsmanlike, and they hate dead hares."

Then he held me by my hind legs to drain the water out of me, and afterwards began to blow down my nose, I did not know why.

"Don't do that, Tom," said Ella sharply. "It's nasty."

"Must keep the life in her somehow," answered Tom, and went on blowing.

"Master Tom," interrupted Giles, who was rowing the boat. "I ain't particular, but I wish you'd leave that there hare alone. Somehow I thinks there's bad news in its eye. Who knows? P'raps the little devil feels. Any way, it's a rum one, its swimming out to sea. I never see'd a hunted hare do that afore."

"Bosh!" said Tom, and continued his blowing.

We reached the shore and Tom jumped out of the boat, holding me by the ears. The hounds were all on the beach, most of them lying down, for they were very tired, but the men were standing in a knot at a distance talking earnestly, Tom ran to the hounds, crying out—

"Here she is, my beauties, here she is!" whereon they got up and began to bay. Then he held me above them.

"Master Tom," I heard Jerry's voice say, "for God's sake let that hare go and listen, Master Tom," and the girl Ella, who of a sudden had begun to sob, tried to pull him back.

But he was mad to see me bitten to death and eaten, and until he had done so would attend to no one. He only shouted, "One—two—three! Now, hounds! Worry, worry, worry!"

Then he threw me into the air above the red throats and gnashing teeth which leapt up towards me.

The Hare paused, but added, "Did you tell me, friend Mahatma, that you had never been torn to pieces by hounds, 'broken up,' I believe they call it?"

"Yes, I did," I answered, "and what is more I shall be obliged if you will not dwell upon the subject."

THE COMING OF THE RED-FACED MAN

"As you like," said the Hare. "Certainly it was very dreadful. It seemed to last a long time. But I don't mind it so much now, for I feel that it can never happen to me again. At least I hope it can't, for I don't know what I have done to deserve such a fate, any more than I know why it should have happened to me once."

"Something you did in a previous existence, perhaps," I answered. "You see then you may have hunted other creatures so cruelly that at last your turn came to suffer what you had made them suffer. I often think that because of what we have done before we men are also really being hunted by something we cannot see."

"Ah!" exclaimed the Hare, "I never thought of that. I hope it is true, for it makes things seem juster and less wicked. But I say, friend Mahatma, what am I doing here now, where you tell me poor creatures with four feet never, or hardly ever come?"

"I don't know, Hare. I am not wise, to whom it is only granted to visit the Road occasionally to search for some one."

"I understand, Mahatma, but still you must know a great deal or you would not be allowed in such a place before your time, or at any rate you must be able to guess a great deal. So tell me, why do you think that I am here?"

"I can't say, Hare, I can't indeed. Perhaps after the Gates are open and your Guardian has given you to drink of the Cup, you will go to sleep and wake up again as something else."

"To drink of the cup, Mahatma? I don't drink; at least I didn't, though I can't tell what may happen here. But what do you mean about waking up as something else? Please be more plain. As what else?"

"Oh! who can know? Possibly as you are on the human Road you might even become a man some day, though I should not advise you to build on such a hope as that."

"What do you say, Mahatma? A man! One of those two-legged beasts that hunt hares; a thing like Giles and Tom—yes, Tom? Oh! not that—not that! I'd almost rather go through everything again than become a cruel, torturing man."

As it spoke thus the Hare grew so disturbed that it nearly vanished; literally it seemed to melt away till I could only perceive its outline. With a kind of shock I comprehended all the horror that it must feel at such a prospect as I had suggested to it, and really this grasping of the truth hurt my human pride. It had never come home to me before that the circumstances of their lives—and deaths—must cause some creatures to see us in strange lights.

"Oh! I have no doubt I was mistaken," I said hurriedly, "and that your wishes on the point will be respected. I told you that I know nothing."

At these words the Hare became quite visible again.

It sat up and very reflectively began to rub its still shadowy nose with a shadowy paw. I think that it remembered the sting of the salt water in the cut made by the glass of the window through which it had sprung.

Believing that its remarkable story was done, and that presently it would altogether melt away and vanish out of my knowledge, I looked about me. First I looked above the towering Gates to see whether the Lights had yet begun to change. Then as they had not I looked down the Great White Road, following it for miles and miles, until even to my spirit sight it lost itself in the Nowhere.

Presently coming up this Road towards us I saw a man dressed in a green coat, riding-breeches and boots and a peaked cap, who held in his hand a hunting-whip. He was a fine-looking person of middle age, with a pleasant, open countenance, bright blue eyes, and very red cheeks, on which he wore light-coloured whiskers. In short a jovial-looking individual, with whom things had evidently always gone well, one to whom sorrow and disappointment and mental struggle were utter strangers. He, at least, had never known what it is to "endure hardness" in all his life.

Studying his nature as one can do on the Road, I perceived also that in him there was no guile. He was a good-minded, God-fearing man according to his simple lights, who had done many kindnesses and contributed liberally towards the wants of the poor, though as he had been very rich, it had cost him little thus to gratify the natural promptings of his heart.

Moreover he was what Jorsen calls a "young soul," quite young indeed, by which I mean that he had not often walked the Road in previous states of life, as for instance that Eastern woman had done who accosted me before the arrival of the Hare. So to speak his crude nature had scarcely outgrown the primitive human condition in which necessity as well as taste make it customary and pleasant to men to kill; that condition through which almost every boy passes on his way to manhood, I suppose by the working of some secret law of reminiscence.

It was this thought that first led me to connect the new-comer with the Red-faced Man of the Hare's story. It may seem strange that I should have been so dense, but the truth is that it never occurred to me, any more than it had done to the Hare, that such a person would be at all likely to tread the Road for many years to come. I had gathered that he was comparatively young, and although I had argued otherwise with the Hare, had concluded therefore that he would continue to live his happy earth life until old age brought him to a natural end. Hence my obtuseness.

The man was drifting towards me thoughtfully, evidently much bewildered by his new surroundings but not in the least afraid. Indeed there none are afraid; when they glide from their death-beds to the Road they leave fear behind them with the other terrors of our mortal lot.

Presently he became conscious of the presence of the Hare, and thoughts passed through his mind which of course I could read.

"My word!" he said to himself, "things are better than I hoped. There's a hare, and where there are hares there must be hunting and shooting. Oh! if only I had a gun, or the ghost of a gun!"

Then an idea struck him. He lifted his hunting-crop and hurled it at the Hare.

As it was only the shadow of a crop of course it could hurt nothing. Still it went through the shadow of the Hare and caused it to twist round like lightning.

"That was a good shot anyway," he reflected, with a satisfied smile.

By now the Hare had seen him.

"The Red-faced Man!" it exclaimed, "Grampus himself!" and it turned to flee away.

"Don't be frightened," I cried, "he can't hurt you; nothing can hurt you here."

The Hare halted and sat up. "No," it said, "I forgot. But you saw, he tried to. Now, Mahatma, you will understand what a bloodthirsty brute he is. Even after I am dead he has tried to kill me again."

"Well, and why not?" interrupted the Man. "What are hares for except to be killed?"

"There, Mahatma, you hear him. Look at me, Man, who am I?"

So he looked at the Hare and the Hare looked at him. Presently his face grew puzzled.

"By Jingo!" he said slowly, "you are uncommonly like—you are that accursed witch of a hare which cost me my life. There are the white marks on your back, and there is the grey splotch on your ear. Oh! if only I had a gun—a real gun!"

"You would shoot me, wouldn't you, or try to?" said the Hare. "Well, you haven't and you can't. You say I cost you your life. What do you mean? It was my life that was sacrificed, not yours."

"Indeed," answered the Man, "I thought you got away. Never saw any more of you after you jumped through the French window. Never had time. The last thing I remember is her Ladyship screaming like a mad cockatoo, yes, and abusing me as though I were a pickpocket, with the drawing-room all on fire. Then something happened, and down I went among the broken china and hit my head against the leg of a table. Next came a kind of whirling blackness and I woke up here."

"A fit or a stroke," I suggested.

"Both, I think, sir. The fit first—I have had 'em before, and the stroke afterwards—against the leg of the table. Anyway they finished me between them, thanks to that little beast."

Then it was that I saw a very strange thing, a hare in a rage. It seemed to go mad, of course I mean spiritually mad. Its eyes flashed fire; it opened its mouth and shut it after the fashion of a suffocating fish. At last it spoke in its own way—I cannot stop to explain in further detail the exact manner of speech or rather of its equivalent upon the Road.

"Man, Man," it exclaimed, "you say that I finished you. But what did you do to me? You shot me. Look at the marks upon my back. You coursed me with your running dogs. You hunted me with your hounds. You dragged me out of the sea into which I swam to escape you by death, and threw me living to the pack," and the Hare stopped exhausted by its own fury.

"Well," replied the Man coolly, "and suppose I, or my people, did, what of it? Why shouldn't I? You were a beast, I was a man with dominion over you. You can read all about that in the Book of Genesis."

"I never heard of the Book of Genesis," said the Hare, "but what does dominion mean? Does this Book of Genesis say that it means the right to torment that which is weaker than the tormentor?"

"All you animals were made for us to eat," commented the Man, avoiding an answer to the direct question.

"Very good," answered the Hare, "let us suppose that we were given you to eat. Was it in order to eat me that you came out against me with guns, then with dogs that run by sight, and then with dogs that run by smell?"

"If you were to be killed and eaten, why should you not be killed in one of these ways, Hare?"

"Why should I be killed in those ways, Man, when others more merciful were to your hand? Indeed, why should I be killed at all? Moreover, if you wished to satisfy your hunger with my body, why at the last was I thrown to the dogs to devour?"

"I don't quite know, Hare. Never looked at the matter in that light before. But—ah! I've got you now," he added triumphantly. "If it hadn't been for me you never would have lived. You see I gave you the gift of life. Therefore, instead of grumbling, you should be very much obliged to me. Don't you understand? I preserved hares, so that without me you would never have been a hare. Isn't that right, Mr.—Mr.—I am sorry I have forgotten your name," he added, turning towards me.

"Mahatma," I said.

"Oh! yes, I remember it now—Mr.—ah—Mr. Hatter."

"There is something in the argument," I replied cautiously, "but let us hear our friend's answer."

"Answer—my answer! Well, here it is. What are you, Man, who dare to say that you give life or withhold it? You a Lord of life, you! I tell you that I know little, yet I am sure that you or those like you have no more power to create life than the world we have left has to bid the stars to shine. If the life must come, it will come, and if it cannot fulfil itself as a hare, then it will appear as something else. If you say that you create life, I, the poor beast which you tortured, tell you that you are a presumptuous liar."

"You dare to lecture me," said the Man, "me, the heir of all the ages, as the poet called me. Why, you nasty little animal, do you know that I have killed hundreds like you, and," he added, with a sudden afflatus of pride, "thousands of other creatures, such as pheasants, to say nothing of deer and larger game? That has been my principal occupation since I was a boy. I may say that I have lived for sport; got very little else to show for my life, so to speak."

"Oh!" said the Hare, "have you? Well, if I were you, I shouldn't boast about it just now. You see, we are still outside of those Gates. Who knows but that you will find every one of the living things you have amused yourself by slaughtering waiting for you within them, each praying for justice to its Maker and your own?"

"My word!" said the Man, "what a horrible notion; it's like a bad dream."

He reflected a little, then added, "Well, if they do, I've got my answer. I killed them for food; man must live. Millions of pheasants are sold to be eaten every year at a much smaller price than they cost to breed. What do you say to that, Mr. Hatter? Finishes him, I think."

"I'm not arguing," I replied. "Ask the Hare."

"Yes, ask me, Man, and although you are repeating yourself, I'll answer with another question, knowing that here you must tell the truth. Did you really rear us all for food? Was it for this that you kept your keepers, your running dogs and your hunting dogs, that you might kill poor defenceless beasts and birds to fill men's stomachs? If this was so, I have nothing more to say. Indeed, if our deaths or sufferings at their hands really help men in any way, I have nothing more to say. I admit that you are higher and stronger than we are, and have a right to use us for your own advantage, or even to destroy us altogether if we harm you."

The Man pondered, then replied sullenly—

"You know very well that it was not so. I did not rear up pheasants and hares merely to eat them or that others might eat them. Something forces me to tell you that it was in order that I might enjoy myself by showing my skill in shooting them, or to have the pleasure and exercise of hunting them to death. Still," he added defiantly, "I who am a Christian man maintain that my religion perfectly justified me in doing all these things, and that no blame attaches to me on this account."

"Very good," said the Hare, "now we have a clear issue. Friend Mahatma, when those Gates open presently what happens beyond them?"

"I don't know," I answered, "I have never been there; at least not that I can remember."

"Still, friend Mahatma, is it not said that yonder lives some Power which judges righteously and declares what is true and what is false?"

"I have heard so, Hare."

"Very well, Man, I lay my cause before that Power—do you the same. If I am wrong I will go back to earth to be tortured by you and yours again. If, however, I am right, you shall abide the judgment of the Power, and I ask that It will make of you—a hunted hare!"

Now when he heard these awful words—for they were awful—no less, the Red-faced Man grew much disturbed. He hummed and he hawed, and shifted his feet about. At last he said—

"You must admit that while you lived you had a first-class time under my protection. Lots of turnips to eat and so forth."

"A first-class time!" the Hare answered with withering scorn. "What sort of a time would you have had if some one had shot you all over the back and you must creep away to die of pain and starvation? How would you have enjoyed it if, from day to day, you had been forced to live in terror of cunning monsters, who at any hour might appear to hurt you in some new fashion? Do you suppose that animals cannot feel fear, and is continual fear the kind of friend that gives them a 'first-class time'?"

To this last argument the Man seemed able to find no answer.

"Mr. Hare," he said humbly, "we are all fallible. Although I never thought to find myself in the position of having to do so, I will admit that I may possibly have been mistaken in my views and treatment of you and your kind, and indeed of other creatures. If so, I apologise for any, ah—temporary inconvenience I may have caused you. I can do no more."

"Come, Hare," I interposed, "that's handsome; perhaps you might let bygones be bygones."

"Apologise!" exclaimed the Hare. "After all I have suffered I do not think it is enough. At the very least, Mahatma, he should say that he is heartily ashamed and sorry."

"Well, well," said the Man, "it's no use making two bites of a cherry. I am sorry, truly sorry for all the pain and terror I have brought on you. If that won't do let's go up and settle the matter, and if I've been wrong I'll try to bear the consequences like a gentleman. Only, Mr. Hare, I hope that you will not wish to put your case more strongly against me than you need."

"Not I, Man. I know now that you only erred because the truth had not been revealed to you—because you did not understand. All that I will ask, if I can, is that you may be allowed to tell this truth to other men."

"Well, I am glad to say I can't do that, Hare."

"Don't be so sure," I broke in; "it's just the kind of thing which might be decreed—a generation or two hence when the world is fit to listen to you."

But he took no heed, or did not comprehend me, and went on—

"It is an impossibility, and if I did they would think me a lunatic or a snivelling, sentimental humbug. I believe that lots of my old friends would scarcely speak to me again. Why, putting aside the pleasures of sport, if the views you preach were to be accepted, what would become of keepers and beaters and huntsmen and dog-breeders, and of thousands of others who directly or indirectly get their living out of hunting and shooting? Where would game rents be also?"

"I don't know, I am sure," replied the Hare wearily. "I suppose that they would earn their living in some other way, as they must in countries where there is no sport, and that you would have to make up for shooting rents by growing more upon the land. You know that after all we hares and the other game eat a great deal which might be saved if there were not so many of us. But I am not wise, and I have never looked at the question from that point of view. It may seem selfish, but I have to consider myself and the creatures whose cause I plead, for something inside me is telling me now—yes, now—that all of them are speaking through my mouth. It says that is why I am allowed to be here and to talk with you both; for their sakes rather than for my own."

"If you have more to say you had better say it quickly," I interrupted, addressing the Red-faced Man. "I see that the Lights are beginning to change, which means that soon the Road will be closed and the Gates opened."

"I can't remember anything," he answered. "Yes, there is one matter," he added nervously. "I see, Mr. Hare, that you are thinking of my boy Tom, not very kindly I am afraid. As you have been so good as to forgive me I hope that you won't be hard on Tom. He is not at all a bad sort of a lad if a little thoughtless, like many other young people."

"I don't like Tom," said the Hare, with decision. "Tom shot me when you told him not to shoot. Tom shut me up in a filthy place with a yellow rabbit which he forgot to feed, so that it wanted to eat me. Tom tried to cut me off from the wood so that the running dogs might catch me, although you shouted to him that it was not sportsmanlike. Tom dragged me out of the sea and blew down my nostrils to keep me alive. Tom threw me to the hounds, although Giles remonstrated with him and even the huntsman begged him to let me go. I tell you that I don't like Tom."

"Still, Mr. Hare," pleaded the Red-faced Man, "I hope that if it should be in your power when we get through those Gates, that you will be merciful to Tom. I can't think of much to say for him in this hurry, but there, he is my only son and the truth is that I love him. You know he may live—to be different—if you don't bring some misfortune on him."

"Who am I to bring misfortune or to withhold it?" asked the Hare, softening visibly. "Well, I know what love means, for my mother loved me and I loved her in my way. I tell you that when I saw her dead, turned from a beautiful living thing into a stained lump of flesh and fur, I felt dreadful. I understand now that you love Tom as my mother loved me, and, Man, for the sake of your love—not for his sake, mind— I promise you that I won't say anything against Tom if I can help it, or do anything either."

"You're a real good fellow!" exclaimed the Red-faced Man, with evident relief. "Give me your hand. Oh! I forgot, you can't. Hullo! what's up now? Everything seems to be altering."

As he spoke, to my eyes the Lights began to change in earnest. All the sky (I call it sky for clearness) above the mighty Gates became as it were alive with burning tongues of every colour that an artist can conceive. By degrees these fiery tongues or swords shaped themselves into a vast circle which drove back the walls of darkness, and through this circle, guided, guarded by the spirits of dead suns, with odours and with chantings, descended that crowned City of the Mansions before whose glory imagination breaks and even Vision veils her eyes.

It descended, its banners wavering in the winds of prayer; it hung above the Gates, the flowers of all splendours, Heaven's very rose, hung like an opal on the boundless breast of night, and there it stayed.

The Voice in the North called to the Voice in the South; the Voice in the East called to the Voice in the West, and up the Great White Road sped the Angel of the Road, making report as he came that all his multitude were gathered in and for that while the Road was barred.

He passed and in a flash the Gates were burned away. The ashes of them fell upon the heads of those waiting at the Gates, whitening their faces and drying their tears before the Change. They fell upon the Man and the Hare beside me, veiling them as it were and making them silent, but on me they did not fall. Then, from between the Wardens of the Gates, flowed forth the Helpers and the Guardians (save those who already were without comforting the children) seeking their beloved and bearing the Cups of slumber and new birth; then pealed the question—

"Who hath suffered most? Let that one first taste of peace."

Now all the dim hosts surged forward since each outworn soul believed that it had suffered most and was in the bitterest need of peace. But the Helpers and the Guardians gently pressed them back, and again there pealed, no question but a command.

This was the command:—

"Draw near, thou Hare."

Jorsen asked me what happened after this justification of the Hare, which, if I heard aright, appeared to suggest that by the decree of some judge unknown, the woes of such creatures are not unnoted and despised, or left unsolaced. Of course I had to answer him that I could not tell.

Perhaps nothing happened at all. Perhaps all the wonders I seemed to see, even the Road by which souls travel from There to Here and from Here to There, and the Gates that were burned away, and the City of the Mansions that descended, were but signs and symbols of mysteries which as yet we cannot grasp or understand.

Whatever may be the truth as to this matter of my visions, I need hardly add, however, that no one can be more anxious than I am myself to learn in what way the Red-faced Man, speaking on behalf of our dominant race, and the Hare, speaking as an appointed advocate of the subject animal creation, finished their argument in the light of fuller knowledge. Much also do I wonder which of them was proved to be right, a difficult matter whereon I feel quite incompetent to express any views.

But you see at that moment I woke up. The edge of the Road on which I was standing seemed to give way beneath me, and I fell into space as one does in a nightmare. It is a very unpleasant sensation.

I remember noticing afterwards that I could not have been long asleep. When I began to dream I had only just blown out the candle, and when I awoke again there was still a smouldering spark upon its wick.

But, as I have said, in that spirit-land wither I had journeyed is to be found neither time nor space nor any other familiar thing.

H. Rider Haggard – A Short Biography

Sir Henry Rider Haggard, KBE was born on June 22nd, 1856 at Bradenham in Norfolk, England.

More familiarly known as H. Rider Haggard, he was the eighth of ten children born to Sir William Meybohm Rider Haggard, a barrister (born, incidentally, in St Petersburg, Russia), and Ella Doveton, an author, poet and daughter of a merchant in the East India Trading Company.

Haggard was initially schooled at Garsington Rectory in Oxfordshire where he studied under the tutelage of Reverend H. J. Graham. His elder brothers, who seemed to find more favour with their father, graduated from various private schools whilst Haggard was sent to Ipswich Grammar School, saving his father a considerable sum in fees.

He failed his army entrance exam, and was therefore sent to a private crammer in London in preparation for the entrance exam to the British Foreign Office, which he appears never to have sat. However, it was during his two years in London that Haggard came into contact with a circle of people interested in the study of psychical phenomena and for which he too now developed a life-long interest together with a series of enduring friendships.

In 1875, Haggard's father used his family's connections to send him to Southern Africa to take up an unpaid position as assistant to the secretary to Sir Henry Bulwer, Lieutenant-Governor of the Colony of Natal. In 1876 he was transferred to the staff of Sir Theophilus Shepstone, Special Commissioner for the Transvaal. It was in this role that Haggard was present in Pretoria in April 1877 for the official announcement of the British annexation of the Boer Republic of the Transvaal. The official who had been nominated to read out the Proclamation lost his voice and Haggard was his replacement. It was a moment in history.

Haggard was to remain in the country for six years, during which time he served as Master of the High Court of the Transvaal and an adjutant of the Pretoria Horse.

It was here that he fell in love with Mary Elizabeth "Lilly" Jackson. He hoped to marry her once he obtained more certainty in his career path.

In 1878 he became Registrar of the High Court in the Transvaal and now the time seemed opportune to write to his father to tell him of his hope to marry. The reply from his father was uncompromising. He forbade it until his son had made a proper career for himself.

The following year, 1879, Lily married Frank Archer, a well-to-do banker.

Haggard returned briefly to England to marry a friend of his sister's, Marianna Louisa Margitson, a 21 year old, in 1880, and the couple travelled to Africa together. Haggard's years in Africa had proved, at least on a writing level, rich and inspirational for him, and while still in Natal he wrote two articles for The Gentleman's Magazine describing his experiences.

Moving back to England in (and accounts here differ as to whether it was 1881 or 1882) the couple settled in Ditchingham, Norfolk, Louisa's ancestral home. Later they moved to Kessingland and established connections with the church in Bungay, Suffolk. The marriage produced four children. A son named Jack (who tragically died at age 10 of measles) and three daughters, Angela, Dorothy and Lilias. (Lilias grew to become an author and her father's biographer.)

In England Law was to be the fulcrum of his career. However, although he studied, writing was growing in its appeal to him. His first book, Cetywayo and His White Neighbours, was an account and study of Britain's policies in South Africa.

From this point his career as a writer began to take substantial hold and with it a dramatic shift to fiction. Two years later he published his first fiction, Dawn followed in 1885 by arguably his most popular novel, King Solomon's Mines—detailing the life of the adventurer Allan Quatermain. This was followed the following year, 1886, by She: A History of Adventure, which introduced the female character Ayesha. Both characters, Quatermain and Ayesha, developed a series of books about their adventures.

The study of Law now fell away entirely. He appeared also to have a keen sense of his commercial appreciation. Rather than sell the copyright of his first best-seller, King Solomon's Mines, for a £100 fee he, instead, accepted a 10% royalty. This book is also generally accepted as the first of the Lost World writing genre.

Haggard obviously thought there were many further adventures to tell and it would be hard to find a publisher who would disagree given the start he had made. Sequels soon followed. Allan Quatermain continued his epic and swash-buckling adventures in Africa whilst the sequel to She entitled Ayesha played out her adventures in Tibet. Interestingly Haggard would later extend his characters adventures around the world with Eric Brighteyes, being the basis for an epic Viking romance.

The Haggard family lived at 69 Gunterstone Road in Hammersmith, London, from mid-1885 to mid-1888. It was here that he wrote his most famous works. His time in Africa had given him the experience and atmosphere as well as several observations and friendships of the people who would so influence his fictional characters. Chief among them were the larger-than-life adventurers Frederick Selous and Frederick Russell Burnham. Both were men of Empire and huge ambition as they helped uncover the great mineral wealth of Africa, as well as the ruins of ancient lost civilisations of the continent, such as Great Zimbabwe.

Three of Haggard's books, The Wizard (1896), Black Heart and White Heart; a Zulu Idyll (1896), and Elissa; the Doom of Zimbabwe (1898), are dedicated to Burnham's daughter Nada, the first white child born in Bulawayo; she had been named after Haggard's 1892 book Nada the Lily.

As is typical of the writing of the time his novels contain many of the stereotypes associated with colonialism, yet they also sympathise, to a degree, with the native populations. Africans often play heroic roles in the novels, although the protagonists are more often than not European. The time around the turn of the century was, after all, the great sprint to Empire by many European countries intent on gaining possessions of land, people and resources.

Three of Haggard's novels were written in collaboration with his friend Andrew Lang who shared his interest in the spiritual realm and paranormal phenomena and who was also a greatly admired editor.

Haggard's stories are still widely read today. Ayesha, the female protagonist of She, has been cited as a prototype by psychoanalysts such as Sigmund Freud (in The Interpretation of Dreams) and Carl Jung. Her epithet is, of course, "She Who Must Be Obeyed" and has for decades been used tongue-in-cheek to describe the presumed balance of influence between the sexes.

As a legacy it is easy to establish Haggard, and his pioneering work, as the author of the Lost World branch of writing and its influence of such other writers as Edgar Rice Burroughs, Robert E. Howard and Talbot Mundy. The Allan Quatermain character influenced many 'serials' in Hollywood during the 30s & 40s and can readily be seen as a template for Indiana Jones, the American archaeologist and explorer and huge box office film character.

Years later, when Haggard was a successful novelist, he was contacted by his former love, Lilly Archer, née Jackson. Lily had been deserted by her husband, who had embezzled funds and fled bankrupt to Africa. Haggard installed her and her sons in a house and saw to the children's education. Lilly eventually followed her husband to Africa, where he infected her with syphilis before dying of it himself. Lilly returned to England in late 1907, where Haggard again supported her until her death on April 22nd, 1909.

Haggard also wrote about agricultural and social reform, in part inspired by his experiences in Africa, but also based on what he saw in Europe. By the end of his life, he was adamantly opposed to Bolshevism, a position that he shared with his life-long friend Rudyard Kipling. The two had found friendship upon Kipling's arrival at London in 1889 largely on the strength of their shared opinions.

Haggard was extremely interested in the social affairs of the Country and eager to play a more active part in attempting reform. In 1895 he stood unsuccessfully for Parliament as a Conservative candidate for the Eastern division of Norfolk losing by 198 votes.

Also in 1895 he served on a government commission to examine Salvation Army labour colonies. This, and his heavy involvement in agriculture reform, led to him being a member of several further commissions on land use and related affairs, work that involved several trips to the Colonies and Dominions. This work, in part, helped lead to the passage of the 1909 Development Bill.

In 1911 he served on the Royal Commission examining coastal erosion.

He was an absorbed and dedicated writer of letters to The Times, nearly one hundred were published by them and the bibliography attached below reveals much in the range of subjects he wished to bring attention to.

He was made a Knight Bachelor in 1912 and a Knight Commander of the Order of the British Empire in 1919. Haggard was a member of several clubs including the Athenaeum, Savile, and Authors' clubs.

The district of Rider in British Columbia, Canada, was named in his honour.

Henry Rider Haggard died on May 14th, 1925 at the age of 68. His ashes were buried at Ditchingham Church. His papers are held at the Norfolk Record Office.

The first chapter of his book People of the Mist (1894) is credited with inspiring the 1912 motto of the Royal Air Force (formerly the Royal Flying Corps), Per ardua ad astra. "Through adversity to the stars" (or alternately "Through struggle to the stars") it is also used by other Commonwealth air forces such as the RAAF, RCAF, RNZAF, and the SAAF.

H. Rider Haggard – A Concise Bibliography

Novels
Dawn (1884) Published in three volumes
The Witch's Head (1884) Published in three volumes
King Solomon's Mines (1885) Allan Quatermain series
She: A History of Adventure (1886) Ayesha series
Allan Quatermain (1887) Allan Quatermain series
Jess (1887)
A Tale of Three Lions (1887) Allan Quatermain series

Maiwa's Revenge, or the War of the Little Hand (1888) Allan Quatermain series
Colonel Quaritch, VC (1889) Published in three volumes
Cleopatra (1889)
Beatrice (1890)
The World's Desire (1890) Co-written with Andrew Lang
Eric Brighteyes (1891)
Nada the Lily (1892)
An Heroic Effort (1893)
Montezuma's Daughter (1893)
The People of the Mist (1894)
Heart of the World (1895)
Joan Haste (1895)
The Wizard (1896)
Doctor Therne (1898)
Swallow: A Tale of the Great Trek (1899)
Lysbeth (1901)
Pearl Maiden (1903)
Stella Fregelius: A Tale of Three Destinies (1903)
The Brethren (1904)
Ayesha: The Return of She (1905) Ayesha series
The Way of the Spirit (1906)
Benita (1906)
Fair Margaret (1907)
The Ghost Kings(1908)
The Yellow God (1908)
The Lady of Blossholme (1909)
Morning Star (1910)
Queen Sheba's Ring (1910)
Red Eve (1911)
The Mahatma and the Hare (1911)
Marie (1912) Allan Quatermain series
Child of Storm (1913) Allan Quatermain series
The Wanderer's Necklace (1914)
The Holy Flower (1915) Allan Quatermain series
The Ivory Child (1916) Allan Quatermain series
Finished (1917) Allan Quatermain series]
Love Eternal (1918)
Moon of Israel (1918)
When the World Shook (1919)
The Ancient Allan (1920) Allan Quatermain series
She and Allan (1921) Allan Quatermain series / Ayesha series
The Virgin of the Sun (1922)
Wisdom's Daughter (1923) Ayesha series
Heu-Heu (1924) Allan Quatermain series]
Queen of the Dawn (1925)
The Treasure of the Lake (1926) Allan Quatermain series
Allan and the Ice-Gods (1927) Allan Quatermain series
Mary of Marion Isle (1929)

Belshazzar (1930)

Short Story Collections

Allan's Wife and Other Tales (1889)
Black Heart and White Heart: A Zulu Idyll (1900)
Smith and the Pharaohs (1920)

Publications in Periodicals and Newspapers

A Zulu War-Dance (July 1877) The Gentleman's Magazine
A Visit to the Chief (September 1877) The Gentleman's Magazine
Hydrophobia (letter) (3 November 1885) The Times
The Land Question (letter) (28 April 1886) The Times
About Fiction (February 1887) The Contemporary Review
Mr Rider Haggard and His Critics (letter) (27 April 1887) The Times
Our Position in Cyprus (July 1887) The Contemporary Review
American Copyright (letter) (11 October 1887) The Times
On Going Back (November 1887) Longman's Magazine
Delagoa Bay (letter) (17 December 1887) The Times
South African Policy (letter) (27 December 1887) The Times
Suggested Prologue to a Dramatised Version of She (March 1888) Longman's Magazine
Mr. Meeson's Will (18 June 1888) The Illustrated London News
The Wreck of the Copeland (18 August 1888) The Illustrated London News
Cleopatra (3 December 1888) The Illustrated London News
Hydrophobia and Muzzling (letter) (25 October 1889) The Times
The Annals of Natal (23 November 1889) The Saturday Review
Mummy at St Mary/Woolnoth's (letter) (25 December 1889) The Times
Mummies (letter) (27 December 1889) The Times
The Fate of Swaziland (January 1890) The New Review
In Memoriam (17 May 1890) Thompson's Seasons
American Copyright (letter) (5 June 1890) The Times
Mr Herbert Ward and Mr Stanley (10 November 1890) The Times
Nada the Lily (2 January 1892) The Illustrated London News
A New Argument Against Creation (19 December 1892) The Times
My First Book. Dawn. By H. Rider Haggard (April 1893) The Idler
The Tale of Isandlwana and Rorke's Drift (4 October 1893) The True Story Book
Lobengula (letter) (19 October 1893) The Times
The New Sentiment (letter) (6 November 1893) The Times
Wanted—Imagination   (25 December 1893) The Times
The Fate of Captain Patterson's Party (28 December 1893) The Times
The Three Volume Novel (letter) (27 July 1894) The Times
The Adventures of John Gladwyn Jebb (letter) (30 October 1894) The Times
Agriculture in Norfolk (letter) (30 October 1894) The Times
The Nelson Bazaar (letter) (16 February 1895) The Times
Everything is Peaceful (letter) (20 March 1895) The Times
Lord Kimberley in Norfolk (letter) (17 April 1895) The Times
The East Norfolk Election (letter) (23 July 1895) The Times

The East Norfolk Election (letter) (29 July 1895) The Times
Wilson's Last Fight (7 October 1895) The True Story Book
The Crisis in the Transvaal (letter) (2 January 1896) The Times
The Transvaal Crisis (letter) (13 January 1896) The Times
Jameson's Surrender (letter) (14 March 1896) The Times
The Rinderpest in South Africa (letter) (5 November 1896) The Times
Mr Rider Haggard and Dr Neufeld (letter) (9 January 1899) The Times
Shrinkage of Population in Agricultural Districts (letter) (9 May 1899) The Times
The South African Crisis—An Appeal (letter) (1 July 1899) The Times
Commandant-General Joubert and Mr H Rider Haggard (letter) (8 September 1899) The Times
Anglo-African Writers' Club (17 October 1899) The Times
The War (letter) (25 October 1899) The Times
Farming in 1899 (letter) (22 December 1899) The Times
Farming in 1899 (letter) (1 January 1900) The Times
Settlement of Soldiers in South Africa (letter) (5 May 1900) The Times
1881 and 1900 (letter) (2 October 1900) The Times
Farming in 1900 (letter) (1 January 1901) The Times
Central and Associated Chambers of Agriculture (letter) (6 November 1901) The Times
Small Holdings (letter) (8 November 1901) The Times
Rural England (letter) (4 February 1903) The Times
Mr Rider Haggard on Rural Depopulation (3 May 1903) The Times
Agricultural Distress (letter) (11 June 1903) The Times
The Motor Problem (letter) (24 June 1903) The Times
Fiscal Policy and Agriculture (letter) (16 December 1903) The Times
Telepathy Between a Human Being and a Dog (letter) (21 July 1904) The Times
Telepathy Between a Human Being and a Dog (letter) (9 August 1904) The Times
Mr Rider Haggard on Small Holdings (12 September 1904) The Times
Case L.1139 Dream (October 1904) Journal of the Society for Psychical Research
Mr Rider Haggard on Agriculture (22 October 1904) The Times
Mr Rider Haggard on Rural Housing (27 October 1904) The Times
The Deserted Village (letter) (25 August 1905) The Times
Decrease of Population and the Land (letter) (6 January 1906) The Times
Prevention of Cruelty to Children (3 February 1906) The Times
The New Land and Tenure Bill (letter) (12 March 1906) The Times
Garden City Association (17 March 1906) The Times
Mr H. Rider Haggard on the Zulus (19 May 1906) The Illustrated London News
To Be Proof against British Bullets: A Zulu Incantation (19 May 1906) The Illustrated London News
Housing of the Working Classes (26 June 1906) The Times
Mr Rider Haggard on Small Holdings (4 July 1906) The Times
The Unemployed and Waste City Lands (letter) (19 July 1906) The Times
Mr Rider Haggard on the Transvaal Constitution (7 August 1906) The Times
Vanishing East Anglia (1 September 1906) The Saturday Review
The Land Grabbing at Plaistow (5 September 1906) The Times
The Land Tenure Bill (22 November 1906) The Times
Publishers and the Public (letter) (19 February 1907) The Times
The Careless Children (2 March 1907) The Saturday Review
The Government and the Land (letter) (29 April 1907) The Times
Chambers of Agriculture (2 May 1907) The Times

Sir R Haggard's Tour. Land for Ex-Service Men (22 July 1916) The Times
Sir H. Rider Haggard's Mission. Land for Ex-Soldiers (1 August 1916) The Times
Land for Ex-Soldiers. Outline of Sir R. Haggard's Report   (12 August 1916) The Times
Empire Land Settlement Deputation to the Secretary of State for the Colonies and the President of the
Board of Agriculture (September 1916) United Empire
Empire Land Settlement by Sir Rider Haggard (December 1916) United Empire
A Journey through Zululand by Sir H Rider Haggard (December 1916) The Windsor Magazine
Mr Wilson's Note. British Publicity (28 December 1916) The Times
Home Produce (letter) (22 February 1917) The Times
The Milk Supply (letter) (11 April 1917) The Times
Corn Production Bill. A National Measure (letter) (13 June 1917) The Times
A Protest and a Plea. Farmers and Meat (letter) (9 October 1917) The Times
Pig-Breeding. A Subject for Municipal Enterprise (letter) (22 February 1918) The Times
The German Colonies. Interests of the Dominions (letter) (5 November 1918) The Times
Light—More Light! (letter) (19 November 1918) The Times
A Great American. Tributes to the Late Mr Roosevelt (letter) (8 January 1919) The Times
Shut the Door (letter) (10 March 1919) The Times
Population and Housing. Emigration v Birth Control (25 March 1919) The Times
The Ex-Kaiser (letter) (11 April 1919) The Times
Empire Birth-Rate. Sir Rider Haggard on Emigration (17 April 1919) The Times
Ex-Service Men Abroad. Warnings from California (letter) (10 May 1919) The Times
Edith Cavell (letter) (16 May 1919) The Times
The Ex-Kaiser. Uncertainties of Trial (letter) (8 July 1919) The Times
Race Suicide Peril. Western Civilization Threatened (11 October 1919) The Times
The British Cinema. Production of Reputable Films (letter) (5 November 1919) The Times
Horrors on the Film. Limits of Publicity (letter) (19 November 1919) The Times
The British Museum (letter) (24 January 1920) The Times
Air Exploration and Empire (letter) (7 February 1920) The Times
The Liberty League. A Campaign Against Bolshevism (letter) (3 March 1920) The Times
Bolshevist Peril. Counter-Propaganda (4 March 1920) The Times
The Empire's Vacant Lands. Settlers and the Food Supply (14 April 1920) The Times
Films and Happy Endings. The Tyranny of a Convention (letter)   (21 April 1921) The Times
Land and its Burdens. Evil of Grinding Taxation (letter) (8 August 1921) The Times
Boy Emigrants (letter) (31 March 1922) The Times
Migration and Morals. Declining Birther Rate (7 April 1922) The Times
Labour Party's Programme. Confiscation and Class Hatred (letter) (28 October 1922) The Times
Efficient Denmark. Keeping the People on the Land (7 December 1922) The Times
The Egyptian Find. Tombs of Eighteenth Dynasty Queens (letter) (19 December 1922) The Times
King Tutankhamen. Reburial in Great Pyramid (letter) (13 February 1923) The Times
The Norfolk Dispute. A Truce while There is Time (letter) (3 April 1923) The Times
Rural Post and Telephone. Minister's Reply to Deputation (19 April 1923) The Times
Liberalism and Land Reform (letter) (1 May 1923) The Times
Small Holdings. Influence of Heredity (letter) (4 July 1923) The Times
Agricultural Parcel Post (26 July 1923) The Times
Country Houses for Sale. Empty East Anglian Mansions (letter) (14 June 1924) The Times
Plight of Agriculture (24 July 1924) The Times
Loans From the British Museum (letter) (30 July 1924) The Times
Zinovieff Letter. Mr MacDonald and a Political Plot (letter) (29 October 1924) The Times

Two Centuries of Publishing. Tributes to Messrs. Longmans (6 November 1924) The Times
Imagination and War (26 November 1924) The Times

Film Adaptations

King Solomon's Mines

This novel has been adapted at least six times. The first version, King Solomon's Mines, directed by Robert Stevenson, premiered in 1937. The best known version premiered in 1950: King Solomon's Mines, directed by Compton Bennett and Andrew Marton, was followed in 1959 by a sequel, Watusi. In 1979 a low-budget version directed by Alvin Rakoff, King Solomon's Treasure, combined both King Solomon's Mines and Allan Quatermain in one story. The 1985 film King Solomon's Mines was a tongue-in-cheek parody of the story, with a 1987 sequel in the same vein, Allan Quatermain and the Lost City of Gold. Around the same time an Australian animated TV film came out, King Solomon's Mines. In 2008 a direct-to-video adaptation, Allan Quatermain and the Temple of Skulls, was released.

She

She has been adapted for the cinema at least ten times, and was one of the earliest films to be made, in 1899 as La Colonne de feu (The Pillar of Fire), by Georges Méliès. A 1911 version starred Marguerite Snow, a British-produced version appeared in 1916, and in 1917 Valeska Suratt appeared in a production for Fox which is lost. In 1925 a silent film of She, starring Betty Blythe, was produced with the active participation of Rider Haggard, who wrote the intertitles. This film combines elements from all the books in the series.

A decade later another cinematic version of the novels was released, featuring Helen Gahagan, Randolph Scott and Nigel Bruce. Unlike the book and the other films, this 1935 version was set in the Arctic, rather than Africa, and depicts the ancient civilisation of the story in an Art Deco style, with music by Max Steiner.

The 1965 film She was produced by Hammer Film Productions; it starred Ursula Andress as Ayesha and John Richardson as her reincarnated love, with Peter Cushing and Bernard Cribbins as other members of the expedition.

In 2001 another adaption was released direct-to-video with Ian Duncan as Leo Vincey, Ophélie Winter as Ayesha and Marie Bäumer as Roxane.

Dawn

The film Dawn was released in 1917, starring Hubert Carter and Annie Esmond.

Jess

This book was filmed in 1912, featuring Marguerite Snow, Florence La Badie and James Cruze, in 1914 with Constance Crawley and Arthur Maude, and in 1917 as Heart and Soul, starring Theda Bara in the title role.

Beatrice

The book was adapted into a 1921 Italian silent drama film called The Stronger Passion, directed by Herbert Brenon and starring Marie Doro and Sandro Salvini.

Swallow

The novel was adapted into a 1922 South African film.

Stella Fregelius

The book was adapted into a 1921 British film, Stella.

Moon of Israel

This novel was the basis of a script by Ladislaus Vajda, for film-director Michael Curtiz in his 1924 Austrian epic known as Die Sklavenkönigin (Queen of the Slaves).

www.ingramcontent.com/pod-product-compliance
Lightning Source LLC
Chambersburg PA
CBHW071347130626
46556CB00005B/2066